DON'T GO, GORDON

PETER ARMITAGE

Dedicated to the memory of

John Gordon Dickson

CONTENTS

CHAPTER 1

Russia **1917**

The Brigadier

Olga is standing in the street below clapping her hands and stamping her feet to keep the blood circulating. A floral headscarf tied closely over her greying hair serves as a flimsy barrier against the breeze blowing off the bay. There is no telling how long she has been waiting for me to appear. I'm accustomed to being waylaid, with her hand gripped across my arm in a feeble effort to stop me walking away before she spews out every misery that ever befell her. She repeats stories. I have lost count of the number of times her husband has turned purple choking to death on a fish bone and the number of times her firstborn has left her torn inside without any chance of conceiving a second child. She still carries the hurt inflicted by her son who ran away from home to join the navy at the age of sixteen leaving her tormented by visions of his bloated body floating in the icy waters of the Baltic Sea. Olga is angry because the shared toilet is being turned into a stinking sewer by the neighbour's bowel complaint, she is frustrated by the paucity of vegetables to make bortsch, tormented by her chilblains firing up in this cold weather and distressed by reports of young men lying dead on the battlefield far from home. Long lists of gripes and worries settle in her head every night, perched there like a committee of vultures waiting for dawn before flapping around in her brain all day. Whenever her hand pats my forearm I know the rhetorical question is imminent – 'How could the life of a woman who venerates icons many times a day have become so difficult?' We both know her story is commonplace: a deprived childhood, a lonely widowhood, a pious woman facing the end of life with tattered faith and no hope. There are many like her in Vladivostok. She prowls outside hoping for a sympathetic listener but having spotted her from the upstairs front window I leave by the back door. My rent is due today, Olga will have to wait until this afternoon before collecting it.

Svetlanskaya Street is not far from my digs. I work on the first floor of a building here, at a desk facing the only window with an unobstructed view of the hotel entrance across the street. Many of the comings and goings at the Hotel Versailles are routine, my job is to spot and record anything out of the ordinary such as a known prostitute arriving with an unknown client, a newcomer to the city, suspicious groupings of people and anyone dressed in the German style. I collate this information with a list of arrivals and departures supplied to me by a trusted clerk at the front desk before delivering my report to a nameless drop box every day before lunch. I have recently started using red ink to highlight deviations from regular patterns of activity at the hotel, hoping this will facilitate the task of whoever reads the mounds of data submitted for review. That person has called me for an interview today. It will be the first time I can put a name to his face and a face to his name. I expect the meeting will be a painful dressing-down for the unauthorised use of red ink, a sharp reminder that government property shall not be wasted.

There are no pleasantries as I enter. A twitch runs down the fault line in his sagging cheek indicating that I should sit facing him across the narrow desk. He scrutinises me in silence, unaware that I am using the time to make a mental inventory of reasons why his skin colour reminds me of thin pea soup. The most obvious one is a lack of any outside pursuits, typical of overworked bureaucrats, or a liver complaint might be causing such pallor. His voice breaks my train of thought before I reach a conclusion to this trivial question. He is making an awkward attempt to praise my reports without lauding them too much. Expressing his satisfaction with my work is a softening up tactic, his real purpose is to demand more from me.

'I'm unclear whether you are ordering me to extend the hours I spend monitoring the hotel or the quay.'

'Neither. This is about following Somerville to Petrograd,' he replies. 'You will leave next week to deliver an urgent money draft and report back on activity. There is a fast-changing situation up there in the capital.'

The name Somerville is familiar to me, he was a regular at the hotel, but I have not seen him there for over three weeks.

'Sir, I am contracted to the Russo-Asiatic Trading Agency here in Vladivostok from the beginning of November, I cannot go to Petrograd now.'

'Leave that with me. You will take the Great Siberian, arriving there towards the end of the month. Your mission is time sensitive. The last railway workers' strike was broken after only three days, but they might stay out for longer next time. This could be a narrow window of opportunity. Naturally, the inevitable delays caused by sabotage, derailment or repairs on the line are out of our control. In any event the train moves slowly but I can assure you that nothing will get you there faster. You will leave here on Monday 9 October and change trains in Moscow before being met on arrival at the station in Petrograd. Despite the agency's limited funds, soft-class accommodation has been arranged to facilitate several high-level contacts you are expected to make during the journey. Documents will be supplied with a new identity. What name do you propose to adopt, Mr Dickson?'

My face must have gone blank, nothing comes to mind.

'Come on, be sharp,' he commands, stroking his yellowing moustache.

'I will travel as Kenneth Liddell, my younger brother's name,' I reply.

'He's not a Dickson?'

'James Kenneth Liddell Dickson.'

'I don't like the idea of two brothers who share the same name roaming this world.'

'He died in infancy thirty years ago, soon after my eighth birthday.'

'Very well then, Mr Liddell. You have experience in the textile industry I believe.'

I offer to provide references.

'That will not be necessary, I already have the references I need. You will travel as a supplier of Yorkshire cloth to the military and to the imperial household. You are the son of the mill owner, updating your father on business risks and opportunities following the abdication. Your identity allows you to sympathise with any cause, according to need.'

He grunts with satisfaction as I tell him that Liddell is the family name of the woollen and worsted manufacturers at Stanley Mills in Marsh. The words are hardly out of my mouth when a better idea comes to mind. A bulk load of light blue cloth has been ordered for the Tsar's Cossack Regiments from Hainsworth's mill but given the abdication it has not been delivered yet. If cloth for the imperial army is to be part of my backstory, Gordon Hainsworth will be a more credible identity than Kenneth Liddell. Before agreeing to the name change, he wants confirmation that I know Hainsworth products well. I proudly claim knowledge of all the mills within twenty miles of Huddersfield before he shares some unexpected knowledge of his own.

'Hardly surprising I suppose, since you were an apprentice at Acre Mills opposite your father's surgery in Lindley.'

How does he know that much about me? In the brief silence that follows I push my chair out of range of his halitosis, caused either by a serious illness or a foul mix of constipation, cheap cigarettes and ill-fitting dentures still working on the remnants of yesterday's meal.

'Your first report will be from Irkutsk where there is a reliable telegraph service, the next from Ekaterinburg and finally from our embassy on arrival in Petrograd. There should be no other communication except in the case of an emergency. Textile samples on card and several pages of fake correspondence addressed to you from Russian import agents will be provided. Use the reverse side of these documents to write your reports in invisible ink, lemon juice is the most effective but if supplies are not available use your own semen as second best. Every man his own stylo, as we say in the service. Take my advice, make it fresh, Hainsworth, otherwise the paper will stink.'

He pushes his spectacles high up on the bridge of his nose and resumes studying the fact sheet on his desk.

'Born on All Saints. A day of thanksgiving for the lives and deaths of saints both famous or obscure,' he chants as if addressing a class of first-year divinity students. 'For now, you should concentrate on staying alive and obscure, death and sainthood can wait. Born in Beeford, Yorkshire, blue eyes, brown hair, parents both Scottish, six feet tall. Looking at you, I don't think so.'

He uncaps his fountain pen to correct his notes after I confirm my height – five feet seven inches in stocking feet.

'Your identity papers will be ready in forty-eight hours, Mr Hainsworth. Return here to collect them on Thursday at the same hour, there will be a briefing from my colleague at that time. Part your hair on the left and stop shaving from tomorrow, trim your beard lightly before arrival in Petrograd. In addition to the money draft, you will also be carrying embassy mails. You should put all these papers in a satchel and make sure it is safe at all times.'

I ask for his name and that of my contact person during the mission.

'I am known as Brigadier. Your contact will approach you at the appropriate time. He reports to me. Always be on your guard, Mr Hainsworth, you can never be sure to whom you are speaking. You will learn more when you return here on Thursday. A watch with the hands stuck at six o'clock and a wedding ring will be ready for you then, wear them both at all times. If there are no more questions, I bid you good day.'

The signal to leave cannot be clearer but I tarry to catch a glimpse of my surroundings before walking towards the door. The dull oblong office is furnished on three walls with cheap filing cabinets, most of them piled high with bundles of papers, and there is a gilt-framed likeness of King George V hanging askew on the wall opposite the birchwood desk, the only bright note in this unremittingly colourless room. Perhaps it is not the King, it could be his cousin Tsar Nicholas II but no matter, I'm one of many who can't tell them apart. The Brigadier opens his silver cigarette case, lights up, takes a deep draw and nods approvingly at the King, whose eyes are fixed on some far horizon. Studying His Majesty's features closely, he moves to straighten the photograph frame to a precise horizontal, forces the phlegm rising from his throat back down and then turns off the desk light. There is no mistaking this second signal. The meeting is over.

The wall clock, the same make as the one my father has in his surgery, has advanced by less than fifteen minutes as I step outside into an early evening light too weak to cast a shadow. I set off for the park near

Amurskiy Bay, a quiet place to collect my thoughts but change my mind, turn on my heels and head back to my digs to pay Olga. I have always settled my rent on time, she has never had to chase me for arrears but my absence from Vladivostok for a couple of months is sure to make her anxious. It makes me anxious too, I fear she will let her rooms to someone else. I must persuade her to keep the place free for my return, this run-down house has one of the best locations in the city for monitoring shipping movements and ordnance piling up at the harbour. From my bedroom I can see crates being stacked on the quayside, the contents are a mystery but I count them every morning at daybreak as instructed, confident that even such a small contribution to allied intelligence will help us to victory in this wearisome conflict.

Olga will expect to collect three month's rent for my eight-week absence. She is always on the make. As I explain the situation, she tries to confound me with her knit one, purl one, nonsense numbers. With a tip-tap in turn on each of the ten cracked nails poking out of her fingerless gloves, she tots up the length of time her rooms will remain empty before receiving the officially stamped confirmation that I am dead. She tallies the number of weeks following my death in a muddy trench on the front line until the body is formally identified, claiming the process is certain to be prolonged if both my identity tags have been blown away. Then she counts the weeks it will take for a message from the British Embassy overlooking the Neva to arrive in the vice consul's office overlooking Golden Horn Bay, adding a period of unspecified bureaucratic delays for good measure. It is evident to her that the rooms will remain unlet for at least thirteen weeks, during which time rats and damp patches will be free to creep unhindered along the walls of her dingy rooms because nobody will be living there. She rolls back on her broken heels, satisfied with the accuracy of her convoluted calculation, but her triumph is short-lived. As the imaginary death certificate she has been waving in my face wafts down to the pavement, I take her empty hands in mine, peer beyond her cataracts for a dim light that might return my gaze and explain that I'm not going north to fight the Germans. I will not die at the front. Her rudimentary grasp of geopolitics, desperation for cash and maternal instinct break her resolve. The thin wad of notes I have been coaxing into her palm slips away. After an awkward adjustment of her waistband the money disappears somewhere beneath a sheaf of skirts deep in the folds of her bloomers. It is little more than half the amount she was hoping for, but better than waiting to see what tomorrow might bring. Nobody can afford to think long-term these days. We part with her offering profuse thanks – she has never had that much money tucked in her knickers before.

I must reach the tea shop near Nikolai's Triumphal Arch before it closes. I will be sure to find Ling there. I have not yet worked out how to break the news to her that I will be leaving Vladivostok very soon. How can I explain it when I have no idea myself why I have been selected for this assignment?

CHAPTER 2

THE TEA ROOM

I am not a creature of habit or superstitious, but I always take the same route to the tea shop, going around Nikolai's Triumphal Arch rather than passing under it and crossing the main road near the florist where business is slow these days. The breeze blowing from the west fails to raise a hair from under the grip of the Macassar oil I applied this morning, but my pocket handkerchief and tie need small adjustments before I push the door open.

'Sorry, we're closing,' Ling shouts from the back room when the butler's bell, connected to the entrance door by a cord running over pulleys, tinkles excitedly.

'I'll wait here until you open up again in the morning,' I reply, dropping my pitch as far as possible in a feeble attempt to fool her.

'Gordon? Turn the key in the lock, will you?'

Tables and chairs have been moved to the edges of the room, the floor swept clean, the caddies are lined up in their specific places on an eye-level shelf behind the counter, the blue and white tableware, visible through glass panels in the dresser, is neatly arranged and the samovar shines like a half sovereign. Ling appears carrying a small pot of blackcurrant jam cupped in her hands as if it were an offering of ambrosia to the gods. Her collar almost grazes the top button of my waistcoat as she stands facing me, her black eyes trained upwards to a point where they meet a tender response. I bend to kiss her forehead as she raises her heels from the floor.

'Xiao Ling, I'm so happy to see you.'

'Go-Go,' she replies, using a new-found term of endearment, 'I wasn't expecting you here tonight.'

I draw a table and two chairs closer to the centre of the room, bow low and with a flourish invite her to join me for the tea she has started preparing. Too practical to feign a curtsy in response to my faked gallantry, she picks up the jam, spoons a small helping into the bottom of two cups, pours steeped tea from the pot, tops it up with boiling water from the samovar and disappears to find something to eat.

The tea room has a regular clientele whose living standards are boosted rather than diminished by the war. The wives and daughters of local merchants, bureaucrats, and foreign residents can always afford the time and money to while away a whole morning or afternoon here, gossiping over tea unaware that Ling's real business takes place out of sight. She has managed a flourishing Sino–Russian trade from a large, windowless larder adjoining the kitchen ever since her father decided to expand his reach in Imperial Russia. He commands a lucrative share in the huge quantities of tea being shipped through Vladivostok for the army at the front, entrusting Ling to manage this part of his business empire.

She returns with two slices of honey cake. I am not yet ready to announce my imminent departure for Petrograd, it would be too brutal, there must be some small talk first, but Ling is silent. She must sense I have something important to say, what other reason could there be for my unannounced visit? She waits for me to speak. I must weigh the accuracy of every word, I must keep eye contact, I must keep her.

'Why did they choose you?'

'I have no idea,' I reply.

'You are heading into danger again. It will be as bad or worse than the scrape in Ping Yao that almost cost you your life and I will not be there to save you this time. You are mad, Gordon Dickson. Stubborn and mad. Tell them no. Don't go, Gordon.'

'It is my duty to go. King and country.'

'It is not my country and he is not my king.'

'It doesn't work like that Xiao Ling. I'm British, I must go.'

'"You are my queen of hearts", that's what you told me. Your duty is to your queen, not your king. If, by any chance, you don't get killed in Petrograd you will make your way to Scotland alone and I will never see you again.'

'I came to Vladivostok from Kobe because you were here. I promise we will go to Scotland together when my mission to Petrograd is over. We shall get to my grandparents' home in time for Hogmanay.'

'You came to Vladivostok because your job with Abenheim in Japan disappeared when the firm went bankrupt. Be honest, you didn't come here for me.'

'I could have gone anywhere to find work. I chose here because of you.'

'If you want to be with me so much, I will go to Petrograd too. The tea room will survive without me.'

'No, Xiao Ling. This is my work. I must go alone.'

Our eyes no longer meet. Her gaze is fixed on the dark pool of melted jam stuck at the bottom of her cup, mine on the aspidistra in a pot by the door. Silence overcomes us.

My thoughts are drifting back to the day seventeen years ago when I boarded the boat from Wubu County making promises to repay her and her father, Wang Yong, for saving my life. When we parted in that late summer of 1900, I blew a kiss from the deck of the riverboat towards the pontoon jetty where she stood giggling. After placing two fingertips on my lips and blowing the kiss away carelessly on the wind I formed a fragile shell with my hands, covered my mouth with it and housed the second kiss there before releasing it along outstretched fingers on a puff of breath aimed at her. When it arrived, her giggles turned into tears.

I want to make Ling happy. I want to take her to Binniehill House to celebrate Hogmanay in my grandparents' home, to toast the new year and the promise of new beginnings, and to pray with my family that 1918 will not disappoint like all the years since the war started.

Ling is sure to adore my maternal grandmother. Granny Liddell has called me Little Pip for as far back as I can remember – the grandchild she cherishes above all others, the one she said was the apple of her eye, the pip at the core of her greying existence. I nick-named her Granny Smith because her maiden name fits her character so well, she is sharp and sweet at the same time just like the baking apple. We still use these terms of endearment without ever needing to speak of how deeply we care for each other. I know she will still be worrying that my insouciance makes me vulnerable, that people will take advantage of me and I will get hurt. When we meet, she will talk again about the glorious afterlife reserved for her by God in His heaven, the house with many rooms and the promise in John XIV that a place had been prepared and would be waiting for her there. She knows I will need that comfort when the time comes, an antidote to the night-time pain, the inescapable legacy of her death. But that day has not yet come. Soon she will be eighty, exceeding all expectations of longevity, constantly surprised that her Little Pip has become a man with a chestnut brown moustache the same colour as her hair before it turned prematurely white. I have her blue eyes too.

I want to be at Binniehill House in time for her birthday, to see my grandfather, parents and two younger sisters, who will all be gathered there as usual, but sailings from Petrograd are too risky to contemplate. The Gulf of Finland and the Baltic Sea are blockaded by German U boats, which means the only option is an arduous journey through Finland and Sweden before sailing from Bergen across the North Sea to Scotland. I might not be able to get home. In truth I no longer know where home is. My parents had left their ancestral lands shortly before I was born, quitting Scotland for a tiny East Yorkshire village. I don't remember much about Beeford, except a horse and trap were kept in the stable for my father to visit his patients. It was a birthplace, not a home. Scotland might feel like home for as long as Granny Smith is alive, but I have never stayed there long enough for the warmth of the kitchen and its smells, the true test of a home, to make an imprint on my mind.

My memories of Acre Villa are clearer than those of any other place I lived when growing up. It is a short walk from Huddersfield hospital, an imposing property suitable for a Fellow of the Royal College of Surgeons, his wife, three children, a domestic servant, a coachman and a cat. The surgery occupies half the ground floor, it takes precedence over every other room and was strictly out of bounds to me as a boy. The house belonged more to father's patients than to the family that lived there. How could it be home when I was not free to be myself, be free to explore and free to create adventures. Setting foot in the consulting room was forbidden to all except my mother and the maid whose presence was tolerated only for dusting and the provision of tea on demand. I often trespassed there to look at anatomical drawings in the vast library of medical books and journals, but it was the specimen jars containing foetuses at various stages of development that fascinated me the most. The jars were lined up high on one of the library shelves, I had to stand on a chair to observe them better. Was this the beginning of life? Had I looked like that before I was born? I remember being lost in thoughts of how bizarre the floating grey shapes looked, especially the malformed specimens, when mother entered without making a noise. She took a firm grip on my ankle, tugged at it until I came down from the chair and in a shrill Scottish accent spoke my name in two menacing syllables. Silence fell across the room and tears rolled down my cheeks as the man I admired and feared in equal measure was called to administer punishment. My father, freshly arrived from the garden, stood mute for a minute before launching a dressing-down more severe than I had been dreading. He never administered corporal punishment, but the scars from his few words, sharper than the rose thorns that had left tell-tale pink scratches running across the back of his hands, were worse. In the adjoining entrance hall, mother scolded Nellie the maid, taking a scalpel to her wages for turning a blind eye to my antics. Nellie's sobbing still echoes when I think of her.

Acre Villa was more like a hospital than a home. The scent of roses and cooking smells should have made it cosy but they were driven out by the stink of carbolic soap and bleach permeating every room. A few months before my sixteenth birthday, father took me out of the suffocating formality reigning inside the house and into the garden to announce that a job had been arranged for me across the road at Acre Mills. At that time, the Sykes family was expanding its production facilities to meet the rising demand for card clothing and hands were being hired to work in the new sheds. I would have the opportunity of learning about the carding process there before starting an apprenticeship with a woollen manufacturer. Doing well and becoming knowledgeable about textiles would open opportunities to travel as a salesman for

Yorkshire cloth, a product known worldwide for its quality. He tried to persuade me that bright young men can make a fine career in the industry. I knew better than to confront him with an outright refusal, but the thought of crossing the road every morning to work at the mill and crossing it again at the end of the day filled me with dread. The routine, the dreariness and the rut that would consume my dreams would be worse than a prison sentence. It would simply be an extension of my unhappy school days. I needed a change of air, a life more exciting than any that could be found in a mill. Had I applied myself better at school there would have been a wider range of openings. I could have studied at Glasgow University, become a doctor like my father and in the fullness of time inherited Acre Villa and its disinfected consulting room, rose beds, bottled unborn babies and its library where Nellie had educated me about how a healthy female foetus, given time, could develop into a beautiful adult body. She treated me to a peep show of pink nipples, buttocks and the quick glimpse of a fuzzy triangle, but it did nothing to encourage me to follow father's footsteps across the messy landscape of human conception, disease and death. I'd rather be out on a muddy rugby field.

My father had been an adventurer himself and knew that any young man with an ounce of spunk awaits a call, any call, to leave home. Immediately after graduating he sailed as a ship's doctor from Scotland to North America with no firm intention of returning. His training was quickly put to the test when several hundred exhausted Icelandic emigrants boarded the SS *St Patrick* in Akureyri and Saudarkrokur en route for

Canada. Many required immediate medical attention. There were illnesses and a broken arm during the voyage, but miraculously the number disembarking in Quebec in September 1874 was the same as those who had embarked two months earlier. There had been one death and one birth during the voyage, nature had been neither mean nor generous. The vessel was decommissioned after its return to Europe and so father found himself back home again, 'The best thing that ever happened to me'. He warned me that it takes desperation and courage to leave home without a return ticket. Those steamship passengers were full of optimism when they looked back for the last time across the waves at the country they were leaving behind. Every passenger carried one small case holding their belongings and a hope that something, anything in North America would be better than the misery they left behind. The seagulls mocked them.

'Stay away from home too long and, like Pompeii, it will have become something unrecognisable by the time you return. Travel the world if you wish but be sure to come back and make a home for yourself here. A man needs roots. There's nowhere better to put them down than here in Yorkshire, God's own country.'

I heard my father's encouragement to discover the world but was deaf to the history of Pompeii.

Ling pulls her fingers away from underneath my hand where they have been sandwiched against the table for long enough. My daydream is over, the corrosive silence breaks.

'I understand,' she says. 'China declared war on Germany only a few months ago. We are on the same side in this conflict, your king is my king, your country is my country. You must do your duty, Go-Go. You must go to Petrograd.'

I tell Xiao Ling how special she is to me, promising to earn enough from this mission to pay our passage from Vladivostok to Europe. A promise of Scotland at the new year, a promise of meeting Granny Smith, a promise of dancing at a ceilidh.

I invite her to rise from the chair, stand to her left, place my right arm behind her neck, my left across my chest, hold her hands and start humming 'Scotland the Brave'.

'This is how we dance the Gay Gordons.'

We march up and down the room, pivot on the spot, take four steps backwards and switch to a lively polka. Ling becomes giddy, she loses her balance and the teacups fly on a reckless journey through the air before smashing on the floor.

'We must practice before I meet your grandmother,' she gasps.

I'm happier than ever to hold her in my arms. We hug tighter, finally peeling apart to say farewell, our eyes gleaming beneath mounting tears. We will not see each other again before I leave for Petrograd, her time is taken managing a tea empire that grows faster than the Tsar's empire crumbles. She stands outside on the pavement, her back as straight as a topgallant mast, her head held as proud as an ensign, watching me walk away. Before rounding the corner, I turn again to look back at her and blow a Wubu-style kiss, but she has disappeared inside to lock up.

CHAPTER 3

Cʜɪɴᴀ 1900

Ling's Story

I went back inside my shop before he vanished round the corner because I could not bear to prolong the parting. This separation has hurt me more than when I stood on the jetty facing Wubu County seventeen years ago watching him sail away. I was young at that time and had no deep attachment to him but now the plans we have made for a life together have been put in jeopardy. Gordon was stubborn and unfathomable earlier, talking incessantly about his duty, doing the right thing and following orders without question. Am I to believe that his duty is a higher priority than our future? I hate the thought that we are being forced apart by some functionary called the Brigadier who sits in the safety of his office issuing commands that put Gordon in danger. I would rather us die together in Petrograd than be abandoned here alone. Gordon's fears for my safety are misplaced because I feel resilient enough to face whatever would have awaited me in Petrograd. Generations of my family have survived hardship and I am no different.

My father, Wang Yong, has arrived from China and will stay here for a week to review business operations, meet with customers and agents, and attend briefings on the political situation from his trusted sources. Plans for a proper office must be agreed with him. It is impossible for me to function effectively from the small space next to the kitchen, there is no natural light, the desk is too small to open more than one ledger at a time and the filing shelves are full. But Yong will probably want to reconfigure the layout of the rooms behind the tea shop at the lowest possible cost rather than rent additional space. He is cautious about spending more money than necessary in case political change puts the future of his Russian operations at risk. Growing up through the toughest of times has made him self-sufficient and wary.

He lived through the great famine when every family affected by it suffered deprivation and the loss of loved ones. When I was old enough to understand, he told me stories about his life, how the people in the northern provinces of China were reduced to eating carrion and roots in a hopeless attempt to stay alive. How his parents had sacrificed their own chances of survival by feeding their only son all the precious scraps they could find. How they died in agony after refusing one of the only remaining sources of food – boiled children. My father, then a scrawny thirteen-year-old orphan, was led away from the packs of dogs tearing at putrefying human flesh lying unburied along the roadside, from the smell of death, by his uncle. It was the second month in the year of the Red Fire Ox when they headed south-eastwards across arid land

and dry riverbeds to escape from starvation and pestilence. Ensnaring a ring-necked pheasant or a wild hare fed their fantasies, but it was mostly stolen eggs, plain wheat cakes, wizened pomegranates, roots bulked up with clay and thin tea that kept them alive on the long trek. Two years later, when the rains came and the crops had started growing again, my father returned to Shanxi province. He was cared for by Christian missionaries who fed, clothed and taught him enough to start an apprenticeship with an ailing tea merchant. This irredeemably sad man had lost all his family to the famine except for the child he gave up in exchange for a sack of millet and everlasting shame. Diminished in strength but mentally agile, the merchant tried to fill the void his bartered son had left behind by taking Yong under his protection and teaching him everything about the tea trade. My father, then a young man full of energy and youthful cunning, developed a talent for buying low and selling high. He learned to keep accurate records of stocks, receivables and payables, to be wary of dubious remittance banks and to keep silver stored in more than one secret hiding place. The master and his apprentice both practised the values taught by the Christian missionaries to whom they owed a debt of gratitude and when the old man's heart summoned up its final weary beat for which it had waited too long, my father inherited the business.

Yong developed the work ethic of a dung beetle. He is a successful businessman but still starts his day early, checking the inward delivery chits, sales dockets and stock levels just as he has done every morning except one – the day I was born. It was Tuesday, the coolies were waiting for Yong's orders to despatch the weekly tea consignment bound for faraway Kyakhta, but he failed to show up. Indifferent to the downpour and to the work waiting for him, he ran through a jumble of muddy streets to fetch his mother-in-law from across town. The contractions had started. The coolies had been kept hanging around for over an hour before Yong appeared. Scurrying between piles of tea bricks stacked on the warehouse floor, shouting instructions from afar, he made sure the shipments were fully loaded before readying himself to join his wife and child as soon as he was called. But the contractions stopped, the call did not come and although the wait would be longer than expected he had good reason to rejoice at the prospect of a delay. He hoped the baby might not be born until the following day, it would be more auspicious, his son would have a better start in life with a birthdate full of lucky numbers to assure him of a long, trouble-free life and exceptional fortune.

Behind the screen, screams were stifled for fear they might attract evil spirits when the baby finally arrived. The expectant father kept returning to spy, listening for tell-tale sounds but hearing only the noise of running water and entreaties to breathe out like a panting dog. At last, a squatting figure, supported by a woman on one side and by a small wooden chest on the other, cast a telling shadow against the calico sheet draped there for privacy. Her waters had broken before midnight and at precisely nine minutes past six the piercing cries of a newborn filled the room. Yong clapped his hands above his head, waiting impatiently for a necklace to be placed on the baby and the umbilical cord to be cut before he would be allowed to draw back the curtain and give his big joy its first bath. My father soon discovered he had been blessed with a little joy not a big one. The son he had hoped for, the firstborn destined to join him in his business, was a daughter. I was born to the sound of wind chimes. My grandfather named me Ling and predicted my destiny. It would be the same as if I had been born a boy – the tea business.

By the time I entered my sixteenth lunar year, I was trusted to sample deliveries from Wuyi Mountain for quality, sort prime leaves picked especially early in the season for the Russian imperial household and check tea bricks delivered from Sichuan province for damage. If too little binding agent had been added to the tea powder or the bricks had not been left long enough to cure, they would crumble and be unsaleable. I supervised the crushing of all the damaged bricks, and the collection of every speck for binding with animal blood and moistening with rice water. The newly pressed bricks, lifted from the moulds and warehoused until hardened were finally packaged in straw and sold by the yak-load to Mongolia and Tibet for a handsome profit. I was soon taking responsibility for dealing with tea merchants, most of them in awe of my acute sense of smell, taste and touch, which they attributed to my auspicious birth date.

As the new century approached, drought and hunger stalked the northern provinces again. Survivors of the great famine feared they would not live through another one, there was no planting or reaping to be done on the hard-baked land. When farm workers were laid off, they occupied their time as best they could by joining the Boxer movement. My father observed the Boxers at the temple, worshipping statues of fake deities veiled in wisps of smouldering incense, and he followed them to the adjoining boxing ground to watch demonstrations of their martial arts prowess and to eavesdrop on the adepts peddling false promises to new recruits. United in righteousness, endowed with special powers and invincible against the enemy barbarians the Boxers resolved to cleanse the land of foreigners and Christians whose devilish methods had poisoned the traditional way of life in the Middle Kingdom. The Boxers claimed they had proof of missionaries standing naked in their rooms at night, wafting their fans by open windows to chase the rain clouds away and prolong the drought. Proof of photographic studios capturing images by using Chinese eyes gouged out and sold to them by foreign devils. Yong knew better than to believe these baseless lies. He refused entreaties to join the Boxer movement, he had no faith in their rituals, he would not enter a trance with them or take on the attributes of their shoddy gods either. They were nothing more than crude copies of heroes from popular novels and imitations of mystical beings incarnated by travelling opera companies.

My father began to worry for our safety, the rabble was becoming more violent and his Christian missionary education was enough to make us a target. There was news of two British missionaries being killed in Yong Qing, churches burnt down, the court declaring war against foreigners and the Dowager Empress herself was reported to be lending support to the Boxers.

In silent moments, Yong shared his growing concerns with my fearless mother although it was almost ten years since she had haemorrhaged to death delivering a stillborn son. He felt her presence. He listened to her guiding spirit counselling him to lie low until the situation calmed down. My father and I had agreed on this strategy, but when the door flew open crashing into a stack of crates and rebounding into the intruder's grimy face, lying low was no longer an option.

'Help me, please help me,' the young man pleaded, gasping for breath.

'You're bleeding, what happened, who are you?'

'I've been attacked. My leg hurts.'

Yong wrapped the man's arm over his shoulder and helped him limp through the warehouse to an uncluttered corner to lay him down on the matting. I ripped his trouser away from the wound, dressed it with sanqi leaves to stem the bleeding, wrapped long strips of clean rags tightly above his knee and tied a knot.

'They're like wild animals. I ditched all the Bibles from my bag and outran them in the alleyways. A band of shouting youths with banners. A lone man appeared from nowhere. He was heading off to join the rioters then spotted me. I thought I was safe, but he headed towards me, attacked using a sharp object then set off to join them, my leg is gashed and blood—'

'Here, drink this and catch your breath.' I wiped his face with a damp cloth before offering him a bowl of lavender tea.

'Where are you going, what are you doing here?' Yong asked.

26

'I'm heading for Taiyuan Fu to join my cousin. She gave me the name of people in Ping Yao, a safe house where I could shelter for a night or two. I was looking for them when I got attacked.'

'Well, Mr Dickson, you've found them,' my father replied.

'How do you know my name?'

'You need to rest.'

My father told me to feed him some jellied bean curd and massage his feet to calm him.

Knowing that a Boxer would not give up the chase once he had the scent of a foreigner, Yong and I pulled a high screen along the length of the matting and dragged five rows of freshly filled brick moulds across the floor, laying them in a compact rectangle against the screen to prevent anyone approaching it. Gordon stirred. I arranged his deflated Gladstone bag as a pillow and urged him to stay silent. I helped my father to push a large tank on wheels across the approach to Gordon's feet, and after climbing a stepladder he filled a small pail from the tank and set it down on the floor. I did not understand his plan until he took a ladle, dipped it in the bucket and spread animal blood over the trail of stains left by Gordon's injured leg. By this time, Gordon had fallen into a deep sleep, oblivious to chants of 'Drive out foreigners, kill Christians,' coming from the street. Nothing would be gained by wakening him, he would learn of the news from Taiyuan Fu sooner rather than later. Even a scrawny young man shouting at Yong failed to disturb Gordon.

'You are hiding a foreigner here,' the words landed on my father's face in a spray of furious spittle.

'You are mistaken,' he replied calmly.

'I struck him hard, this is his blood on the floor.'

'That is animal blood, not human blood.'

'What animals do you kill here?' the Boxer mocked, banging his wooden staff too close to Yong's feet.

'Not one animal is slaughtered here. There was a delivery of blood just before you arrived, we use it to make tea bricks. The dumb coolies over-filled their buckets, slopping blood on the floor before they even got as far as the storage tank. Those uneducated idiots don't care.'

'Show me.'

'My daughter will show you, she makes the tea bricks,' Yong replied.

'No contact with women, I want no contact with women. It is forbidden for Boxers.'

'Come with me then. Look in that tank, check. If you find a foreigner, I'll give you food. Here, take your staff, give it a stir,' Yong shouted as the Boxer hooked his arms over the rim, preparing to peer into the still, henna-coloured depths, eager to corner his prey.

As soon as he looked up, but before he could extend an arm to grab the pole, Yong forced his head down with it and kept his nose and mouth submerged until the small body stopped twitching.

We squatted, facing each other across Gordon's outstretched leg as he stirred from his slumber. Yong insisted we wait for him to be fully awake before starting to slurp down a large bowl of pork and celery dumplings floating in a mixture made with vinegar and spices. We shared the food with Gordon but kept the news from Taiyuan Fu to ourselves, he still had no inkling of the drama that had unfolded there.

When we had finished eating I stitched up the rent in his trousers. It was too painful for him to have them touching his injury so my father lent him a loose knee-length tunic. The foreign devil was dressed like a local.

'I must leave tomorrow. I'm expected at the mission. They will be disappointed I had to jettison the Bibles.'

'You must not go, Mr Dickson,' Yong advised him.

'You are still in need of treatment,' I insisted, knowing it would be reckless for him to leave so soon. The camphor-leaf compresses would have to be applied over several days to disinfect the wound properly.

'Your hospitality is much appreciated. You have been kind. I've lost time and my cousin is waiting. She will take care of me until I recover fully.'

My father could no longer delay.

'There is bad news from Taiyuan Fu, Mr Dickson.'

'What kind of news?'

'Your cousin ...'

'Christina?'

'Yes, Christina.'

'What?'

'I am sorry to tell you, she is dead.'

'No, it can't be. Not that, please not that.'

'There has been a massacre. Governor Yu-Hsien ordered the missionaries beheaded.'

'Beheaded?' Gordon repeated the word in disbelief.

'On the ninth of this month, many people were killed.'

'Her husband, William? A son was with them. Are they safe?'

'All dead, Mr Dickson. All dead.'

'Why would they kill a doctor? The boy, he was just a wee laddie. Don't tell me they beheaded him?'

'Wee laddie?'

Neither Yong nor I understood.

'A boy, a young boy.'

'These are abnormal times. You are lucky to be alive, children were beheaded too.'

'Alexander was barely ten years old. I attended his parents' wedding in Falkirk a few weeks before my eleventh birthday, about the age he is now. I must go north quickly to give them a decent burial.'

'If you go, you will be killed, Mr Dickson. Too late now. Some bodies were thrown outside the city walls and left for the dogs. Chinese Christians tried to bury them at night, they were caught and beheaded the following day.'

'The Lord help us.' Gordon put his hands together in prayer. 'My poor Uncle Alec and my aunt, will they know their grandson and his parents are dead?'

'It only happened last Monday. The news may not have reached England yet.'

'Scotland, they live in Scotland,' Gordon mouthed in a dazed voice.

'We know about Scotland. There are good engineers from Scotland here in China.'

'My uncle was not an engineer. He was a grocer and the postmaster in Slamannan.'

'Slamannan is Glasgow? Big ships are built in Glasgow. It is a very famous place.'

'No, Slamannan is not Glasgow. It's a small village about twenty miles away.'

'South?'

'No, east towards Edinburgh,' Gordon replied, but Yong and I were lost, wandering around somewhere far away from Slamannan on our imaginary map of Great Britain.

Gordon dragged his injured leg into position, crouched in a bear cub pose, haunches in the air, gave a mighty push and stood upright on the matting. Turning his face towards the wall to disguise his emotions with a forced sneeze, his eyes turning watery and even redder than before, he began pacing up and down exercising his leg for the first time since it had been slashed open. He was considering his options. He decided to travel by night, head for the port of Tianjin, board a steamship and work his passage home. He had not finished explaining his plans before my father interrupted him.

'No, too dangerous.'

'I must get home, I must comfort Christina's parents, I must see the two children they left behind in Scotland.'

'I understand, Mr Dickson, but listen to my advice, your plan is a bad one.'

'My father and I want you to travel with a tea consignment leaving here for the port of Shanghai. I will accompany you.'

'You must not go near Tianjin, it's unsafe in the north.'

'I cannot put Ling in danger. Helping a foreigner, her life would be at risk.'

'My life will not be in danger, I have my mother's jade talisman. Who will challenge me?

31

The Boxers avoid women. I know the carters, the safe stopping places, the inns, the boatmen, the trustworthy people along the way. I have done the journey before. You will be hidden in a tea chest until we reach safer territory. We will travel in the heat of the day when the Boxers are at rest, when it is too hot for rioting. We leave next Tuesday, the biggest day of the week for shipments from the warehouse, our departure will not arouse any suspicion.'

'You spend two or three days in the chest pretending to be a tea leaf then it will be safe to come out,' Yong added, making light of the risks. 'You will be close to Wubu County by then, after that there are no more Boxers. You will follow the Yellow River to the south, cross to Huai'an then down the Grand Canal towards Shanghai where you can board a steamship for London.'

'Shanghai, my first view of China. It seems such a long time ago, so much has happened.'

When the time came for Gordon to leave, Hsi-en, who helped at the warehouse most days, made the necessary preparations. He stacked wooden frames with tea bricks, manoeuvred them onto the coolies' backs, examined the straw casings, tightened the straps and stood back to check that the pyramid-shaped loads were securely tethered. The coolies stood in a long line in the lane outside the warehouse, leaning on their staves, knees bent under their heavy burdens, waiting for the first one to break rank and set off for the inn where the tea bricks would be handed over to long-distance haulers. As they stood there, rooted like a row of trained pear trees, Gordon climbed onto a cart drawn up behind them. Shielded from prying eyes, safe behind the impenetrable barrier formed by the coolies' loads, he twisted every limb to fit himself into a perforated box. Hsi-en had knocked it together from two tea chests and I stocked it with enough victuals for the day. The coolies set off whilst the other tea chests were being loaded, I took my place on the cart and prodded the horse to take its first hesitant steps towards the west. Hsi-en drew his mare to the mounting block, lowered the wicker baskets that were hanging too high against her flanks, took a firm grip on the halter and walked alongside the cart. His face was impassive, but I know he was proud that my father trusted him to make the journey with me.

Gordon must have felt the cart being pulled away from the warehouse with a sudden jerk before it settled down into a slow, rhythmic jostle as the horse found its stride. Unable to see anything through the air holes punched in the side of the tea chest, he was as isolated and vulnerable as a farm animal being taken to slaughter. The perilous forty-eight hours ahead, in rising heat and humidity, were made as tolerable as possible. Zhu sha pills calmed him and liquorice reduced his urine output. I used traditional medicine to ensure my cargo would stay docile and dry. When we reached a safe inn the cart rattled through the courtyard to a remote corner where it would stay overnight, unseen from the street. Hsi-en jumped down from his mount, tethered both animals to brass rings before watering them and joined the innkeeper, who was telling me in hushed conversation about a band of Boxers roaming in the vicinity. It was too dangerous to let Gordon out of the tea chest. Hsi-en dossed down on the cart, snoozing fitfully under a purple sky, a bad omen sure to trouble him more than he would ever admit. Shortly before dawn I appeared from the shadows signalling to Hsi-en that Gordon should slink out of his box and follow me to a hiding place close by. As we crept away, the innkeeper approached carrying two wriggling rabbits, skinny specimens hanging by their ears, their eyes bulging like ripe grapes as he tossed them roughly into Gordon's vacated habitat. Hsi-en watched in silence, twiddling the end of his queue as he always did when the world made no sense to him.

'What is your business here?'

The courtyard had filled with young men, a mud-slide of humanity seeking a purpose in life. Gordon and I could see them from our hideaway behind an animal pen where pigs, hens, rabbits and their cocktail of smells shared a rickety structure of wood and wire cages. I could sense restlessness in the Boxer's ranks, an itch for action, a sense of urgency to impale a foreign head on a stake before the sun appeared above the horizon. Hsi-en, alone on the cart, shook nervously as the crowd surrounded him. He had grasped the meaning of the purple sky. Death.

'I am delivering tea from Ping Yao to Wubu County,' he replied, summoning up as much confidence as he could find.

'We control commerce through here, get down. The tea chests will be examined.'

The young men split into groups, each tasked with checking an item on the cart. One chest after another was lifted down and opened with a crowbar. Whilst the

Boxers rummaged through the contents satisfying themselves that nothing other than tea leaves was inside, Hsi-en busied himself by replacing the lids. He would have to provide an explanation for the extra-large chest, the last one to be inspected.

'What is this?' the leader of the mob demanded, leaping onto the cart. 'Why is it twice the size of the others? What are the air holes for? You're hiding a foreigner in here.'

The men cheered, banged their staves on the ground and pressed forward to see the chest as it was about to be manhandled.

'Don't take this one down,' the group leader commanded. 'It will be opened on the cart so everyone can see the foreign devil crawl out, piss himself and have his head removed.'

Bending low, arms akimbo with a machete slung across his back, he dragged out each word as he repeated in a menacing voice, 'Piss himself and have his head removed.'

Making a grand gesture, he pried the chest open with a crowbar thrown up from the crowd.

'I breed rabbits,' Hsi-en explained before being asked the question. 'There were twenty-four when I set off. I've sold twenty and eaten two.'

The Boxer grabbed the animals, pulled them out and dangled them both in front of his jeering comrades.

'I planned to keep these two but can sell them to you,' Hsi-en said respectfully, not wanting to fuel any anger.

'Sell? We do not buy, we take,' the Boxer mocked, looking down at both miserable animals swinging by their back legs from his left hand.

With a well-aimed blow, the Boxer struck one rabbit on the back of its head with the crowbar and tossed the lifeless body into the crowd, to the sound of excited cheers. The next blow landed badly, the second animal twitched and had to be despatched in a bloody spray of clobbering.

'Rabbits,' he said flinging his head back in laughter. 'Next time we take your whole consignment and you will leave here empty handed.'

The filthy youths were good humoured, they had seen blood.

Gordon held me close as we listened to events unfolding in the courtyard. Our greatest fear, that the Boxers would hang around searching and eventually corner us, never came to pass. Spilling blood and humiliating Hsi-en had satisfied their immediate needs. The call to false idol worship and martial arts practice sucked the danger out of the courtyard, away from Gordon and towards the boxing ground. The innkeeper beckoned us inside. Gordon's injured leg had gone stiff after squatting too long, his shirt was wet with perspiration and my heart pounded with a confusing combination of relief and unfamiliar feelings for the man who had been protecting me in his arms.

'Seize this opportunity, go immediately,' the innkeeper told Gordon. 'You will get into the hills before they leave the boxing ground. Ling must return to her father, Hsi-en will take you to Wubu County.'

'No, I will take Mr Dickson. Hsi-en, prepare the cart, leave the rabbits' box in place, erect panels around it leaving a void that you will fill with muck. Make sure a mound of manure covers the top of the box. Leave a corridor of clean space behind where I sit, open only to the sky, for a man to lie there foetus-like.'

'Ling, your father is my dear friend. I must look after you. Hsi-en will go, you will stay.'

'You will look after the tea chests, Hsi-en will look after himself and I will look after Mr Dickson. Taking care of my friend is more important than returning to my father, besides nobody will trouble a woman driving a cart load of shit.'

Then Gordon spoke, 'The Dickson motto is *Fortune Favours the Brave,* I will go with Ling not Hsi-en.'

CHAPTER 4

THE GREAT SIBERIAN 1917

I do not possess a formal dinner suit, smoking jacket, spare boots or other items considered essential for the journey. The agency has borne the cost of filling a trunk with them and sending everything directly to the luggage wagon. The ring is on my wedding finger, the watch stuck at six o'clock is on my wrist, I finished packing the Gladstone bag a few minutes ago, and the diplomatic bag is tucked tightly under my arm. Even though it is only a short distance to the railway station, the tram pulling up alongside me will be faster than walking. I've made the wrong choice climbing aboard. The brakes squeal and the tram comes to a halt as the road ahead is blocked by a crush of soldiers, silent mourners and a group of rowdy dockers heading homewards after their shift. Time is short. My dealings with Olga took much longer than expected, the only option is to jump off the tram, dash between the horse-drawn hearse and the grieving widow hobbling behind it, then dodge through the crowds. One grand leap beneath the central arch without putting a foot on the steps saves me a few precious seconds, elbowing my way through the masses in the passenger hall saves a few more. The belt of my winter coat is trailing along the floor behind me but there is no time to thread it back through the loop it has escaped from, that will have to wait until later. I cannot spot the silhouette of the Great Siberian through clouds of steam, but I hear it. The sound of its whistle blows a hole in my guts, the train must be pulling out already, I have just missed it and just lost my job. But now I'm closer I realise it is not moving, that was only the first whistle, there are two more before the chuntering giant leaves Vladivostok with me on board.

The butler, troubled by condensation forming on the left lens in his spectacles, is forced to cock his head slightly to read my travel documents. After taking a cursory glance at them and without speaking a word he leads me down the corridor to my soft-class accommodation. The elegant compartment, the music room, library, first-class dining room and a veloroom for physical exercise will be my home for the next three weeks. I have Russian wide-gauge tracks to thank for the extra-long couch, and French design for the finely upholstered armchair and elaborate curtains, the stylish marble washbowl and the stock of soaps and fragrances. I know not which guardian angel has transported me from Olga's dingy rooms into this shameless luxury. Ling would feel uncomfortable in these sumptuous surroundings, but I will have no difficulty adapting to them. How I would love Granny Smith to see me now.

The butler is a man of few words, his Russian delivery is so fast that I have trouble understanding him. I cannot be sure whether he just confirmed that my trunk is in the luggage wagon and will be delivered to my compartment within the hour or it has gone missing. I have the answer when I open the wardrobe and find my clothes hanging there. The young, stocky man will be acting as butler to the occupants of this carriage and the adjoining one for the entire journey. He seems aloof unless my first impressions of him are mistaken. His spectacle lens is still clouded over, the condensation should have cleared by now, it must be permanently opaque. He is either covering up an eye injury or he has been discharged from the army with the highly infectious trachoma that is rife amongst soldiers. There are no tell-tale watery secretions from his grey eyes, but I shall keep my distance from him, make my own bed and fold my own towels to lessen the risk of catching the disease myself.

A money draft made out in my name for fourteen thousand roubles to be lodged with the Russo-Asiatic Trading Agency on arrival in Petrograd, the sealed wallet containing the mail of His Majesty's Embassy for hand-delivery to the Ambassador's private secretary and the four thousand roubles on account of my commission are safely locked away in my bag. The small bronze key is on my albert chain where nobody can touch it without me knowing. I have placed the textile samples and false correspondence from Russian trading firms in the desk drawer opposite the couch. I expect the butler will find them there, he is sure to rummage around in my affairs as soon as the opportunity arises. The on-board staff take bribes for information about travellers, I'm counting on him to find and share my details with all and sundry who will be more likely to believe my identity when it comes from a third source.

The Gladstone bag has been in my possession for years, my father never asked for it back when I returned from China. I have always thought it uncharacteristic of a man who keeps careful track of all his belongings, who wears his lapis lazuli signet ring and engraved gold cufflinks every day, whose spats and cane never go missing. Yet, he must know that the bag bearing his name and gifted to him by his own father at graduation is nowhere to be found. I have never fathomed whether he was so heartbroken after his favourite niece was beheaded that any reminder of the tragedy, including the bag he filled with the Bibles I took to China, was too painful to bear. Or does he secretly want his wandering son to have one of his treasured possessions as a keepsake during his lifetime rather than receive it as a bequest after his death? It has aged. No amount of saddle soap can nourish the scarred leather or hide the scratches, the debossed gold lettering is fading away and the original lock has been replaced by a vulgar but robust substitute. The proud owner, whose name has almost perished in the folds of leather, has been dispossessed by a fiction named Gordon Hainsworth.

At lunch, I hope to identify my contact person. If nobody makes an approach to explain why I'm in this surreal situation I must accept the fact that I am a simple diplomatic courier lucky enough to travel in soft class. The butler, in his customary brusque manner, directs me to a table in the dining car. I shall eat alone facing all the other tables in the carriage with only *The Antiquary* for company. Two ladies sitting at the far end are already finishing their lunch and a gentleman with his back to me has just been served a glass of port. This is not looking promising. Unless he turns around to make a sign or more passengers arrive soon, I will finish dinner without the hope of meeting my contact. I cannot imagine either of the ladies is the person I'm looking for. Their easy laughter feeds off a long-established complicity that suggest a mother travelling with her daughter. I can picture my own mother and my sister Connie, not however little sister Gertie who takes life too seriously, delighting in such a meal together albeit with far fewer jewels and much less décolleté on display.

As I finish a plate of delicious cold boiled suckling pig served with horseradish, the ladies leave the carriage in the direction of the music room and the gentleman stands, making steps towards me with the obvious intention of introducing himself. His frame is taller and more athletic than it seemed when he was sitting, waves of thick dark hair are parted as deeply as the Red Sea, his brown eyes shine like the coat of a prize stallion. His pocket handkerchief, stiff collar and flawlessly tailored jacket speak an upper-class language. The man could be five or ten years older than me, of aristocratic birth or just a good imposter. I don't wish to appear jumpy by leaving my seat too early nor disrespectful by rising from it too late, I choose the moment to dab my lips with the stiff white serviette, stand, look him in the eyes and reciprocate his greeting.

'May I introduce myself? My name is Vladimir Bobrov, we shall be travelling companions for the next few weeks. I hope we will have the opportunity to dine together one evening.'

'Sir, it is my pleasure to meet you and I would indeed welcome the opportunity of dining with you. My name is Gordon Hainsworth.' How unfamiliar that name sounds to me when I claim it as my own.

'Mr Hainsworth, I will take my leave and allow you to finish your meal. I shall repair to the smoking room for a cigar, my brother always sends me a box from Davidoff in Geneva for my birthday, and then listen to the concert which will start shortly.'

'Concert?'

'Perhaps I have chosen the wrong word! It is a musical entertainment given by the two ladies who left their table a minute ago. They are travelling to Omsk where the younger one is appearing in a Chekhov play – Masha in *Three Sisters,* I believe. She also sings, accompanied by her mother at the piano. You should attend.'

I think Mr Bobrov clicks his heels before turning to leave but the sound could come from the train passing over a set of points. This might have been a thinly veiled invitation to join him not only for a cigar but also for some informative conversation in the quiet of the smoking corner, but there is not enough time for that before the recital.

People are already seated as I arrive in the music room. The chairs are arranged randomly. I choose one at the back and fix my eyes on the compact grand piano where the elder lady is adjusting the stool. There will be a better opportunity to scan the room when the music begins. A programme of Russian folk songs about peasant life, lost loves, lamentations and invocations is well received with enthusiastic participation during the last song by those members of the audience who know the lyrics. I make a mental note that Vladimir Bobrov sings along like a fish, all bubbles and no words. I also notice that the mezzo-soprano is making repeated efforts to attract my eye, I decide not to telegraph any response but applaud a little more generously than anybody else in the carriage. Others file out first, providing me with a useful moment to study them without anyone made aware of being observed. In addition to Bobrov and the two performers there are three men and one ageing woman whose apparel is more gypsy than duchess. We are all invited to return later in the week when arias from works by Giuseppe Verdi will be performed by a famous member of the State Opera Company who is also travelling to Omsk.

The landscape unfolds at twenty miles per hour, and our first stop at Khabarovsk is due soon. I see fertile plains through the window, a change from the dense forests of birch, beech and evergreens that has been a staple diet since leaving the prairie lands on the plateau above Vladivostok. After almost thirty hours on the train I am itching to leave it for a while. As we pull into the station, noisy waves of hard-class passengers flood onto the platform, pressing forward to get a place at the buffet window, huddling in groups, drinking tea, vodka and kvass, bartering with local traders for milk, hard-boiled eggs, fried morsels, pickled cucumbers and black sour bread. Those travelling in soft class seem to be staying on the train, afraid or unwilling to mix with the unkempt riff-raff down below. I set off alone on a short, refreshing walk down the main boulevard towards the Amur where four turreted gunboats are sheltering, there could be more but I can't see round the bends in the river. Across that wide expanse of water lies China, the land of heartache and joy, violence and love that changed the course of my life. China, the magnet that drew me away from Britain before I could find a wife, found a family, rise to a senior position at the mill and make my parents proud. China sucked me in and spat me out. I feel tempted to try again, to rekindle the old flame, to re-build the broken trust but I must turn my back on China for a second time, make haste for the train and abandon this tranquil spot for the noisy carriage wheels turning, turning, turning on the long iron road leading to Petrograd. The final whistle blows. The butler mumbles a few words to acknowledge my presence on board. I doubt he would care one jot if I had been left standing on the platform.

That walk did not give me enough physical exercise to ensure a good sleep tonight but an hour in the veloroom, exhausting myself on the horizontal bars, pedalling machine, dumbbells and other muscle-toning paraphernalia, should help. There is not enough space for more than two people to use the equipment at the same time, so the butler runs a simple system to avert any disappointments or disputes. Anyone wishing to use the facilities must first hang a red tag on the hook outside his cramped bay. The bath in there is screened off and available only when the butler has been asked politely in advance to fill it with warm water, a time-consuming process given the gigantic tub. I strip down to my full-body underwear and mount the machine barefoot ready to work up a sweat – pedalling the five thousand five hundred miles from here to Petrograd would certainly do the job. I believed myself to be alone, mine was the only tag on the hook, but now after fifteen minutes of vigorous pedalling I hear water splashing in the tub. In a raised voice I enquire who is taking a bath.

'Vladimir Bobrov,' comes the sleepy reply from behind the dividing screen.

'Ah, Mr Bobrov, please excuse me I thought I was alone in this carriage, there was only one tag hanging on the peg.'

'I'm not using the exercise equipment. No tag is needed for sleeping in the bath.'

Mr Bobrov strikes up a conversation. I pedal slowly to concentrate on his every word. He starts by telling me about his family, all the menfolk were sailors as far back as anyone can remember, he never thought about anything other than the navy as a career. Having sailed out of Vladivostok for the past four years he is now returning home to Petrograd where a desk job awaits him. He is as happy with his life as he is with his bath, content with the freedom that bachelorhood brings and optimistic about the future. The war will soon be over, the domestic power struggle will be resolved, soldiers will stop dying, food will become widely available for the masses and the haughty Tsarina will get her comeuppance. A new era is dawning. Sailors, soldiers and railway workers will finally reap their just rewards and aristocrats will no longer dine off banqueting tables dressed by the poor. The railwaymen are some of the most powerful people in the land, they can stop this train and every other train from running for as long as they choose, it happened just a few weeks ago. I listen to him glorifying the common people without inter-rupting his flow, he is persuaded that mutiny by the navy weighs as heavily as strikes by the railwaymen in the current power struggle. I offer no opinion on the matter. It seems bizarre that he would relish the prole-tariat taking power from the elite.

'With or without political views, we all have a rea-son to be on this train, Mr Hainsworth.'

Suddenly, my heart races. His comment invites a response, the first time I will have to speak my false backstory aloud. I have told and retold it in my head many times, convincing myself there is more truth to it than fiction, but will my reason for being on this train sound believable?

'I'll finish my exercise first, then we can talk.'

'Please do, then come and take a bath. It's not often that taciturn butler is in a mood to draw one.'

As I strip off ready to enter the bath, I expect Mr Bobrov to have vacated it, but he is still lounging in the water with both arms hooked across the sides, his man-icured nails beating a cheerful rhythm on the metal rim.

'Climb in, there's room for two. No longer hot but still warm.'

I've taken enough rugby baths not to be fazed by naked male bodies but this, like everything else that has happened to me during the last week, feels pecu-liar. I sit facing him talking about Yorkshire textiles and the cloth that has been ordered for the Tsar's Cossack Regiments.

'Tell your father, he will not get paid. Better keep the cloth in England and find another buyer. Nobody will ever pay the Tsar's bills.'

I lead the conversation away from events in Russia to the safer ground of Scotland, but he doesn't want to linger there.

'Where were you living before arriving in Vladivostok?' he enquires, probing my chronology of events.

'I was shuttling between Yokohama and Kobe working for Abenheim, a German-owned trading company. My time was spent mostly in the foreign concession in Yokohama. The wealthy owner, Mr Abenheim senior, lived with his large family on The Bluff. He was a hands-on manager, always first in the office with a reputation for being the last to leave at night, I saw him often. He invited me to attend two days of celebrations soon after he was awarded the Imperial Honour, it must be about eight years ago now. I traded British textiles for Japanese silk, it was a good business until tariffs were imposed, by 1912 they had impacted trade so badly that cash flow problems brought the company down. That's when I had to leave and return to Britain, my wages stopped being paid when insolvency was declared.'

'If you stayed in Britain working for your father, why did you start this journey in Vladivostok? Surely, you didn't come this far east to catch the Great Siberian going west trying to solve the problem of a few bolts of undelivered cloth?'

'No, of course not. A couple of years after Abenheim's bankruptcy I was called out to Japan again. I had kept in touch with some businesses in the foreign concession, one of them was looking for an experienced trader. If you can trade textiles and silk, you can trade anything, it's the same skill set, just a different underlying product. I expected to stay in Japan longer, but my father telegraphed recently asking me to return home via Russia to collect the kind of intelligence you have just been kind enough to share with me. Vladivostok was the obvious starting point after leaving Japan.'

'Intelligence?'

'Yes, your recommendation not to ship the cloth because we will never get paid for it.'

This is enough cat and mouse talk about my time in Asia. I allow myself to slip down under the water, blow some bubbles as a silly distraction, resurface, shake my hair like a dripping gun dog and change the subject.

'If you want to get a flavour of Scotland, I can recommend reading *The Antiquary,* it's set in the late eighteenth century, it's quite long and much is written in the vernacular but a cracking good story. I finished it during the night, it's back on the library shelf.'

'I wouldn't understand the slang.'

'It has a helpful glossary of Scottish terms.'

'How tiresome.'

'Well, fortunately, there are enough books in the library to suit all tastes.'

'I borrowed *The Picture of Dorian Gray.* Wilde is a more exciting read than boring stories about hot salted porridge and cold Scottish tenements.'

'You treat Scotland very harshly, Mr Bobrov.'

'And you treat Oscar Wilde very harshly.'

'Me?'

'Not you personally, the British. In Russia we cultivate and celebrate artistic flair, in Britain you confine a brilliant writer and thinker to Reading Gaol for two years of hard labour.'

'He broke the law.'

'How absurd. A private, trivial act becomes a public scandal and you imprison a genius. What an outrageous punishment for the love that dare not speak its name.'

His foot slides up my calf, travels across my knee and explores my inner thigh as he quotes Bosie's phrase 'the love that dare not speak its name'. His toes are wiggling. The naval man's engorged periscope has risen above the level of the bath water. I climb out pretending not to have noticed, confidently using the disingenuous reason that the water is turning cold. He ignores my excuse.

'Do not misunderstand me,' he says without a hint of embarrassment. 'I simply had a fascination for that bad scar on your leg, I had an urge to explore it. Please accept my apology, I have shocked you. Scottish Presbyterians are obviously not as tactile as Orthodox Russians.'

There is little doubt about what has just happened, but I tell myself that God has a purpose for every being he has created, perhaps Mr Bobrov's purpose is to tell me my purpose. We will be on the same train for another fifteen days and dining together as early as tomorrow evening, so I decide not to make a fuss about his fumbling.

The dinner with Bobrov is friendly enough, he shares volumes of gossip about people he knows, including the young actress who will be leaving the train at Omsk. Like him, she is looking for a lover. He confesses to having no interest. His table manners, unlike his bathing manners, are impeccable. We talk about Japan. My dining companion is familiar with the washing rituals at the onsen, he displays his knowledge of fine wines, European capitals, Goethe, Racine, Shakespeare and Dostoevsky but knows nothing about rugby. His arrogant charm, refined language and obsessive attention to personal grooming make me doubt his naval background, a subject he refers to repeatedly throughout the meal. My hopes rise briefly when he comments on my watch but rather than telling me it has stopped at six o'clock, he advises me to set it at Petrograd time otherwise I risk being confused by the multiple time zones we shall travel through before reaching our destination. He teaches me about the different qualities of caviar, we sample the best with a generous quantity of vodka which he hopes will loosen my tongue, but I steadfastly decline to take sides. I don't believe his naval background and he doesn't believe I'm in Russia to settle the future of those bolts of blue cloth stored in a Yorkshire warehouse. He asks me to do him the honour of calling him Vladimir, I accept and consequently he now addresses me as Gordon. Despite this new familiarity, our untruths continue to be exchanged with unfailing politeness and conviction. There is still over two weeks for them to unravel.

CHAPTER 5

LESLIE

I stopped shaving the day after leaving my meeting with the Brigadier. My first report to him will be filed by telegraph when we arrive in Irkutsk tomorrow but apart from confirming that my beard is thickening, there is nothing to say. We are almost halfway to Moscow, the view from the carriage is the same hour after hour, mile after mile, wooden hovel after wooden hovel so I have taken to sleeping in the daytime. I stay awake during the nights, they have a magical, mysterious quality. The impenetrable darkness swallows steam from the engine as it wafts close to the windows like a ghost. Nothing else moves in the world beyond, we are alone in the winding gut of this belching monster grinding our way slowly across the freezing dark Siberian plateau thinking only of the next distraction, the next meal. Lake Baikal is somewhere out there tousled by a storm, I have given up hope of seeing it but cross my fingers that fresh fish from the lake will be taken on board at the next stop. The food is less plentiful now. A meagre cutlet was served by the butler yesterday without any explanation for the dearth of vegetables, but vodka and the samovar keep flowing as generously as they have done every day and night since leaving

Vladivostok. I spend an hour or two in the veloroom before dawn, sit at the dining table for long stretches and read whatever books I find in the library but there is nothing exciting to fill my waking hours, nothing of interest to report. I have agreed to teach the pianist, her daughter and Valentina, the slight lady with a complexion like slaked lime, to play whist. I would appreciate some male company, but Vladimir Bobrov is no longer a welcome companion after making a second, cack-handed attempt to seduce me and since the other two gentlemen talk only between themselves, I find myself alone or with female company. The sameness is beginning to weigh on me. I have a vain hope that some new passengers will join this carriage at the next station, but it seems that very few people are travelling towards Petrograd, those who can are fleeing the city.

Valentina spent most of the last evening telling me about her 'gift'. She reads tarot cards, auras and has visions. The waterlogged voice of Rasputin spoke to her in a dream a few weeks ago instructing her to travel by rail from her home in Vladivostok to Tyumen, catch a steamer to Tobolsk, visit the Tsarina there, read the tarot cards and foretell the future of her sickly son, Alexei. Valentina had no second thoughts about following Rasputin's instructions despite the likelihood that the rivers to Tobolsk will already be frozen over, she is confident of success but struggling to interpret the vivid images of the Tsarina who appeared in her dream as the unmarried Princess Alix of Hesse.

'She was taking medicinal waters in a curious little building and bathing in a Moorish interior before removing her sparkling bracelet and proffering it. Where and why?' she asks.

I hold my tongue, there is no joy in humouring Valentina, I might as well let her musings burn themselves out on the embers of her dream. But they don't. I listen politely as she recites at length a tiresome list of continental European spa towns. She names and systematically eliminates those she knows in Germany, Austria, Switzerland, France and Italy, finally settling on somewhere in Spain or North Africa as the most likely place to have a Moorish interior.

'Why do you need to know the precise location?' I ask her. 'Such places don't exist, except in your mind.'

'If I can identify the pump room, the arches, the glazed tiles then the whole content of the dream is affirmed.'

'I don't know if the Princess was ever in Spain or Africa, but I know she came to England. Her mother was English.'

'I know that much about her,' Valentina responded with exasperation. 'How many spa towns do you have in England?'

'I have no idea. Supposing it was not a spa town. It could have been at Osborne House on the Isle of Wight, she is rumoured to have been Queen Victoria's favourite grandchild, so I imagine she went there often.'

'Do people take the waters at Osborne House?'

'The Queen certainly doesn't. She left there in a coffin sixteen years ago.'

Valentina ignores my black humour, dredging more detail from the dream, draining more of my patience.

'I had an image of Princess Alix covering her nose as she takes the water. Why would she show such disgust? Are your English spas dirty and smelly?'

'Harrogate isn't, I don't know any of the others.'

'Harrogate?'

'It's not far from my childhood home, I used to visit a great aunt there when I was about ten years old. In fine weather she took me to play in the Bogs Valley Gardens. We would walk in front of the Royal Baths and I always hid from her outside the pump room, but she was too old to chase me around it.'

'Did your aunt ever tell you much about the interiors?'

'No, she had never been inside. But she loved dawdling by the Royal Baths trying to spot aristocrats or, better still, royalty going in or coming out. She called them the dirtiest folk in Yorkshire because they came to Harrogate to drink smelly mineral water and take mud baths, then she'd chuckle and tell me the Turks wouldn't let them out in town again before they were cleaned up.'

'The Turks?'

'I never understood what she was talking about, I imagined they were fierce soldiers guarding the exits.'

'And the pump room?'

'Octagonal with a strong smell of sulphur pervading the air for a quarter of a mile around.'

'That's it! Turkish baths with a Moorish design, a curiously shaped pump room and the handkerchief protecting against sulphur fumes. Princess Alix was in Harrogate and Harrogate was in my dream. Do you understand how important this is?'

'It fits.'

'Fits? It does more than fit, it confirms, it inspires, it demonstrates my exceptional powers. Do you realise that I have never been to Harrogate, read about it or spoken to anyone who has been there, apart from you and yet I've seen it in my dream?'

'What about the bracelet? You said the Princess took it off,' I quizzed, hoping to fox her.

'It means I will be rewarded with a piece of her jewellery after the reading.'

'Your reading had better tell Alexandra that her beloved son will eventually wear the Great Imperial Crown despite the Tsar having renounced the throne on his behalf too. Otherwise, she will give you nothing.'

Valentina's eyes beam with satisfaction, her joy masked by a hare lip scar that stitches a permanent snarl into her facial expression. She can make the tarot cards say whatever she wants them to say, especially if one of the Tsarina's diamond bracelets is at stake. But the Romanov family has been under house arrest in Tobolsk since August, Valentina will only get access to the lady she hopes to meet by bribing the guards who control her every movement.

At the whist tutorial, Valentina sits to my left, the young singer is opposite me and her mother slides on the empty chair, giggling to herself for arriving late. Although the pair had been introduced formally at the concert of Russian folk songs several evenings ago, the mother insists in a loud voice that she and her daughter should now be addressed by their given names, Yelena and Florentina. I explain the rules of the game, the importance of partners working together to win tricks and the scoring method, but as we play several dummy rounds it becomes apparent that Yelena has not been paying attention. She wastes high-value cards and has not understood the power of trumps, allowing Florentina and me to claim victory every time. Valentina's fingers tap the table in rising frustration at her inept partner before she stands to address Yelena.

'We'll try again when you are sober. Good night.'

'Temperamental witch!' Yelena says under her breath, her giggles turning into deep-throated laughter as Valentina stabs her walking stick, first in the air and then on the floor before disappearing through the freezing rubber booth above the coupling and into the ladies' carriage.

Whist is not a game for three players, so I collect the cards without a plan to fill the silence. It proves to be short-lived. Yelena wants to talk about auras but the only person with any knowledge of them has just departed.

'I so wanted to know about my daughter's aura, she is such a special darling. Her father was Italian, a handsome man with exquisite taste. He was the one who chose the name Florentina, can you imagine anything more feminine? A name that conjures up good-looking women who surround themselves with beauty, women who sing like angels and play-act to rapturous applause. How prescient he was, just look at my daughter now, she is a true Florentina. What a tragedy when he died in the prime of life leaving us to travel the opera houses of Europe without him. Where do I find a suitor good enough for my sweet Florentina? The young men have gone to war, the rich only marry the rich and without a father, my daughter's dowry is …' She stops short of saying 'modest', draws breath and through a tight smile asks, 'What is your business, Mr Hainsworth?'

'Mother, please, you talk too much.'

'I would like you to call me Gordon. I work in the textile industry.'

Yelena quickly stifles a sigh of disappointment as I let drop the lie that my father owns the sole supplier of cloth for Imperial Guard uniforms. Her eyes widen in approval just as I remember that the wedding ring I'm supposed to be wearing is not on my finger, I forgot it by the washstand.

The train comes to a shuddering halt. We are likely to be stationary until morning light when the engineers can fix whatever problem has arisen. We will be late arriving in Irkutsk. If it is minor subsidence affecting the line there should not be too long a delay, anything else could keep us here for days. Ling has been without news from me since we parted, I am anxious to get to our next stop and telegraph to say everything is fine although I miss her terribly. Yelena uses the unexpected halt as an excuse to cure the growing boredom with yet another shot of vodka and in a thinly disguised ruse to leave me alone with Florentina she decides to consult the map of Russia hanging at the far end of the carriage. I make polite conversation about the musical evening and mention her forthcoming stage debut in Omsk.

'I am not leaving the train at Omsk.'

'My apologies. I must have misunderstood Mr Bobrov when he told me that you are appearing in a Chekov play in Omsk.'

Florentina, glossing over the exchange, looks up at the ceiling, her wasp waist arched backwards, her right arm stretched out of a billowing leg of mutton sleeve pointing out the detail of a fresco above us.

'We were admiring the fresco,' she tells her mother who has returned with a refilled glass.

'A fine pastime for young people but I can't possibly look up at the ceiling, it will make me nauseous. It will be a long night. Amuse us Gordon, tell us about your aura. Valentina did read it didn't she?'

Valentina had prefaced yesterday's reading by telling me that the aura gift, transmitted exclusively through the female line, turned up in every second generation of her family. The grandmother who passed on this wondrous poisoned chalice died shortly after Valentina was born, leaving the poor child without anyone to guide her through a lonely adolescence in a world of colours that nobody else could see. Valentina said it was more of a curse than a gift, it revealed more about people than she wanted to know and isolated her from her contemporaries. Dying an old maid to prevent this wretched business from infecting her descendants is not only her wish but also her destiny, like many with Venus in Virgo who never marry. Her real passion is working with tarot cards, reading palms and interpreting dreams, but fearing that any of these could blow my cover I only let her read my aura. I expected it to be straightforward, a dominant colour with a simple explanation, but Valentina sees a perplexing overlap of energies laid almost one on top of the other. A violet-coloured circle with traces of red, encased by an egg shape of cloudy blue with a yolk of lemon yellow made her interpretation so complicated that I barely recognised myself. Don't get a Holy Trinity complex, she warned me, but you are three in one.

'Yes, she read my aura yesterday. My energy field is green, the colour of teachers and healers,' I reply with a straight face.

'Is that all you can tell us? You're a textile salesman not a teacher or healer.'

'Sorry, Yelena, that's it. Nothing more to say.'

'The woman is a complete fraud, all that rice powder on her face, those ridiculous clothes. I'm so pleased she didn't get near my daughter. I feel sure my Florentina radiates magenta and turquoise, such refined, creative colours. I know her energy field so much better than anyone else. I must have a bright red aura myself, driven by passions that cannot always be held in check. Who needs Valentina when we already know the beauty that lies deep within us? Don't you agree, Gordon?'

'Not everybody in the world is as beautiful as you two ladies. I imagine Kaiser Wilhelm has a muddy brown aura.'

'A withered hand too,' Florentina adds disdainfully.

'Always the charmer, always the gentleman,' Yelena says, flattering me before searching for more information. 'I'm surprised you have a green aura. It suggests jealousy.'

'I admit to being jealous when Mr Bobrov told me you are only going as far as Omsk. I'll be stuck on this train for much longer.'

'Don't believe everything Mr Bobrov says,' Yelena whispers before leaning even closer. The lines around her mouth, chiselled deep over many years by inhaling too many cigarettes and infused with the crimson of her lipstick, compress like a concertina about to exhale a secret. Her whispered words 'German spy' are directed more at my eyes than my ears.

The butler has arrived to inform us the train will move again at dawn. The engineer is working throughout the night on a temporary solution to the technical problem, a prolonged stopover in Irkutsk is planned for a more permanent repair.

'I think the butler might have been able to lip-read your words about Bobrov.'

'Butler? Don't be so British, the man is an attendant at best. There will be no jobs for butlers in the new Russia. In any case, he doesn't understand English.'

'We shall have time to visit Irkutsk,' Florentina rejoices.

I'm less interested in looking around the city than I am in locating the telegraph office where I can send a message to Ling. There should be fresh news from the capital too, but I fear it will be bad. The situation there seems to deteriorate further every time reports come in. My immediate intention is to compose a succinct, loving message to Ling. The cost of telegraphing her will be calculated on the number of letters in the message, she should not get the feeling I have made economies, but my budget is limited. I must save enough money for food whenever we make a station stop. The amount served on the train never satisfies my hunger. I had four thousand roubles when we left Vladivostok, almost half has been spent already.

The ladies retire to their carriage as I excuse myself by muttering about working on a business deal, but my real work is composing a message to Ling. After several drafts it finally reads,

> *All OK. Scotland together soon. Gordon loves his Xiao Ling.*

The train has been standing in Irkutsk station no more than fifteen minutes. The attendant, as I now refer to him, presents a sealed telegram addressed to Mister Gordon with a reference number I recognise as that of the railway engine. He is responsible for delivering all mail sent from the telegraph office and held at the station for arriving passengers. It costs me a few precious roubles as I persuade him that despite the absence of a surname, I am the intended recipient. I anticipate reading a cryptic instruction from the Brigadier, but the message could not be more forthright or unexpected.

> *Too dangerous in Russia. Yong sending me back to China. No Scotland. Forget about me. Ling.*

I understand that Yong does not want his daughter exposed to violence in a country with such an uncertain future, but 'Forget about me' is so brutal, so final. Does she really mean it from her heart or am I to believe she is setting me free to head on alone to Scotland without regrets? There will be no answer to this quandary. Screwing up the scrap of paper on which I had carefully drafted my message leaves me feeling empty. My life is drained of any honourable purpose, there must be more to this existence than travelling thousands of miles to deliver a money draft and play whist along the way.

Yelena and her daughter, dressed in boots and full-length golden sable coats with the widest of shawl collars and matching Cossack hats, are readying themselves for a visit to the Church of Our Saviour. Florentina is keen to see the frescoes on the outside walls, light a candle to the memory of her father and look around the new central area of Irkutsk, re-built after the great fire of 1879. I sit in the library, shirt sleeves rolled up, my tweed waistcoat unbuttoned, signalling no interest in their proposal to visit the city together. I need time alone. When the ladies are long gone, I dress for the freezing cold and step out onto the platform to start a brisk walk in the hope it will clear my mind. Nobody tarries. Heads bowed, red cheeks, a specific destination is coded in every step as it crunches on the frosty ground. The air is spotted with clouds of vapour from each panting breath, one is projected across my right shoulder by someone walking too close behind.

'Boyo, your watch is stuck at six o'clock. We need to talk.'

I tug the woollen scarf from across my mouth to reply with a well-rehearsed nonsense phrase which is supposed to elicit a four-word response of special relevance to me. I have been impatient to hear those words since leaving Vladivostok. But whoever spoke to me from behind disappears before I get a chance to turn around and engage in conversation. The approach is aborted.

I fail to recognise Bobrov until he comes close, his features are masked by the side flaps of an ushanka hat pulled down over his ears and the Persian lamb collar on his double-breasted frock coat pulled up above his shoulders. I suspect my contact person fled when he recognised Bobrov before I did, there is no other explanation for such a rapid retreat. Those two must know each other, am I being set up by a pair of German spies operating cat and mouse style to entrap me? Bobrov stands uncomfortably close, clapping his soft leather gloves together to keep his hands warm, suggesting we return to the café in the first-class passenger hall for hot drinks. The idea is tempting but I have no wish to talk to him, especially about what just happened, or ruin my chance of linking up with the contact to complete the coded exchange of our credentials. I bid him farewell, cross the wooden bridge over the Angara River and walk across town before I return to the station without having spoken to anyone. A revised departure time has been posted on the information board. It seems the repairs have progressed faster than expected so the first whistle should be blowing early tomorrow morning. I sit drinking tea in the second-class passenger hall knowing that Bobrov is too much of a snob to enter it, tarrying here before returning to the train, hoping that the mysterious person succeeds in making a second attempt before I board. If not, all is lost.

I sit, watching people come and go, sizing up every individual without staring too much, pacing up and down from time to time to make myself more visible, juggling with the thought that someone will reconnect with me. Fighting off boredom my mind wanders back to my family as it so often does. In my mother's last letter she wrote out the full length of her favourite poem, proudly telling me she had finished a framed sampler of the last two lines. It is now hanging in her home as a constant reminder of what is expected of her four grandsons, one of whom is not yet old enough to read let alone understand 'If'. I cannot help thinking she is using this poem to send a message to me too. The words parade through my mind often, each one surfacing silently with her inimitable imprint taking me back to confusing times when I doubted whether I would ever 'be a man, my son'. My demanding mother is urging me to test myself against the criteria, to look for where I succeed and fail, to remedy my shortcomings. This is not the best of days for assessing whether her son is the man she always wanted him to be.

> *I wait here in this God-forsaken station far from*
> *home but I'm tired by waiting,*
> *I'm lied about but also deal in lies,*
> *dreams of Ling have become my master,*
> *I no longer have the will that says, 'Hold On.'*

I fail to be a man on at least four counts. Damn Kipling.

Working up a sweat on the pedalling machine is about my only hope of staying sane, that failed link-up in Irkutsk is praying on my mind. A unique opportunity lost, wasted like Onan's seed fallen to the ground, because that scene-stealer Bobrov interrupted the connection. There seems little hope of consummating anything now, there are no new faces in the carriage, the person looking for me must be wandering the streets unaware that the train, already twenty minutes out of Irkutsk, departed earlier than expected. I pedal on the machine with an energy driven by frustration, feeling irritable and seeking solitude. There is a shuffling from behind the partition, is Bobrov about? It could be him changing from a smart set of day clothes for an exercise session. I will not vacate the machine for him, he can work out with the barbells or run on the spot until I decide to seek privacy elsewhere. Relieved that he fails to appear, I convince myself he has gone away.

'Boyo, your watch is stuck at six o'clock, we need to talk.'

'Glue in the mechanism, always on Huddersfield time,' I reply, as planned with the Brigadier.

'Yours is the Earth,' comes the agreed response, four of the words embroidered by my mother on the sampler, spoken in a strangely familiar voice.

He steps into the exercise area, smiling broadly. I cannot suppress an open-mouthed double-take. My instinct is to get down but with a hand gesture he bids me stay put on the saddle.

'Sorry this has taken so long,' he says with his arms outstretched, leaning on the handlebar and looking at me, straight in the face.

'You?'

'Yes, me. Surprised?' he replies playfully.

'Supposing Bobrov comes in, he is a regular here.'

'Don't worry. The attendant, the butler as you have been kindly referring to me, has the key to lock carriage doors. We are alone here and will not be disturbed.'

The pedals have stopped turning, perspiration runs in rivulets from my forehead, my trunk is covered in sweat and my waistband soaked in it, but I do not budge apart from dabbing myself with a small towel. He has me spellbound. The man I thought of as taciturn with a command of English no better than a five-year-old child, enthusiastically begins to spill out his story.

His family is the Chandler in Kirkham, Hulett & Chandler, patent holders of washer scrubbers for gas purification. The detail of extracting ammonia, naphthalene, benzol, cyanide and various impurities from coal and other gases is lost on me but now I understand why he is perfectly bi-lingual. By the age of four his parents had left their home in Pontybodkin for London and shortly afterwards they moved to Russia where his father supervised the installation of massive machines manufactured by the family business. Having been educated at the international school in Kiev he can equally well pass as Russian or British, no wonder he has been recruited by the Secret Intelligence Service. Still full of youthful candour, although he must be in his mid-twenties, he talks about his desertion from the navy and a brush with the law at the age of eighteen. How I envy his free spirit, the conservative teachings so liberally spooned out by my mother and her church friends in silly hats made me wary of committing any such misdemeanours. This man sings to his own tune, he is a busker not a chorister.

I listen attentively waiting for some hint that none of this is authentic, Leslie Chandler could be just another alias. But the more he talks, the more I convince myself he is genuine, the impish audacity is real not fake. He speaks convincingly about how the Brigadier arranged his job as an attendant on the Great Siberian where he can spy on soft-class passengers. Leslie accompanied agent Somerville on the train last August supplying him with titbits garnered from conversations in the dining car.

Somerville was running a high fever and when he started coughing up blood Leslie took flight fearing he would catch whatever illness was brewing. He left the train at the first stop and returned to base where he reported back for a briefing on his next mission, describing it as even more important than the previous one.

'Why more important, Leslie?'

'You will learn about it tomorrow. I can promise you excitement, this is not the usual tedious work we do.'

According to Leslie, Somerville was due to meet high-level officials in Petrograd, gather intelligence on the German spy network there and frustrate plans to pull Russia out of the war. My simple task of delivering a money draft is piffling compared to Somerville's assignment. That means the sealed mail of His Majesty's Embassy, safely locked away in my Gladstone bag, must contain something more significant than I had imagined until now. Why else would this mission be more important than Somerville's?

CHAPTER 6

THE LIBRARY

Leslie has asked me to meet him at lunchtime tomorrow in the library, a strange choice given the lack of privacy there. My routine of resting during the day and staying awake at night will have to be reversed to accommodate his request, there is little chance I will sleep tonight but I will give it a try. I make an extra check to ensure there has been no interference with the lock on my Gladstone bag and open the desk drawer to see if the fake correspondence has been disturbed. Nothing is amiss. I decide to seek out Vladimir, he is sure to be smoking a cigar and drinking brandy in the library as he does every evening at around this hour. I will engage him in conversation, share stories about visiting Irkutsk and skate around the subject of the attendant hoping he might be drunk enough to disclose some indiscretions. He must have some knowledge, even one scrap of information that would reassure me about Leslie's true identity. I remember the Brigadier's warning during the interview, 'Always be on your guard, Mr Hainsworth, you can never be sure to whom you are speaking.' How guarded must I be when meeting Leslie tomorrow? Perhaps he will plant some false intelligence knowing I will telegraph it back to Vladivostok at the earliest opportunity, which is still about 2,500 miles down the track in Ekaterinburg. Is the Brigadier himself genuine or a double agent? The more I turn this around in my head, the less sure I am about my next move. The Brigadier was relaxed about my lack of training in espionage, it is now clear to me that he did not want me to have any, but it is proving to be a real handicap. How do I milk information, seed doubt and spot the signs of being double crossed? Who do I trust? Bobrov is certainly untrustworthy, but he is the best source of information about Leslie, he seems to know everything about everyone except me on this train. There would be a better chance of him talking if I let him seduce me, but that would have to happen tonight ahead of the meeting tomorrow and I am not ready to offer up my body for the slim chance of learning more about Leslie. I thought I had understood the situation but on reflection Leslie's story seems too flawless to be true. I shall be extra cautious, more critical tomorrow. Vladimir is nowhere to be found, sleep doesn't come, I'm too busy devising ways of blowing Leslie's cover. A headache takes my left temple hostage, it pounds in unison with the carriage wheels 'Don't go, Go-Go, don't go, Go-Go, don't go, Go-Go'. The samovar is my saviour, tea relieves the headache, but my confidence is unravelling as fast as a skein of yarn just at the moment when the boredom of this journey finally breaks.

One of the gentlemen who attended the concert of Russian folk songs is standing alongside me waiting for his turn to draw water from the samovar. I have never spoken to him despite us being on this train together for what seems to be half a lifetime. He has always been with a companion and neither of them has ever showed any interest in making conversation. They keep themselves to themselves but tonight he is alone, the gossipmongers say the two are in business together planning to make a fortune dealing in Russian artefacts that would reach international markets should the country fall further towards chaos. They are betting on palaces being plundered and the forced sales of precious jewellery, waiting impatiently for the depletion of this country's artistic heritage. A trickle of objets d'art would make them wealthy, a flood would make them fabulously rich. It turns out he can't sleep either. All the compartments in soft class are double occupancy, his insomnia is disturbing the man occupying the other bed. His brother according to Valentina. How fortunate I am to have my compartment to myself. It might not stay that way for the rest of the journey but the chance of someone joining me at this stage of the trip is getting slim.

I plan on making only a polite mumble as he advances to fill his cup, there seems no point in trying to be sociable with a man who never speaks. Surprisingly, he mouths a pleasantry of the kind that hardly calls for a response but rather than ignore it, turn my back on him and return to bed, I stay to drink my tea. The carriage is swaying like a metronome clicking at sixty beats per minute, there is nothing to see beyond the windows, the night is dressed in widow's weeds, the monotony is soporific and defying us to stay awake and talk. He introduces himself, in an accent I cannot place, as Bertram Bridges.

'How far are you going?' he asks.

I bend my well-rehearsed story into a shape that explains why I'm travelling to Petrograd.

'The news from there is bad. Men and horses are dead in the streets, blood staining the snow, stray bullets flying, military hospitals full, food shortages and a hundred new rumours every day. You obviously seek excitement, Mr Hainsworth. I'm leaving the train in Moscow to visit the Fine Arts Museum of Alexander III and one of its benefactors, the Armand family. You must know about them, perhaps you have done business together?'

He is testing my knowledge of textiles.

'Yes, of course,' I reply. 'Their wool-weaving and dyeing factories in Pushkino are well known, I would like to visit them one day.' If I boast of having been there already, he can catch me lying and his trap would spring on me. I set one for him. 'Tell me about the museum collections, I know little about them.'

'The usual. Paintings, sculptures, coins, treasures from ancient Egypt.'

I could have guessed that myself. He fails to offer any details of the collections and I fail to show interest in talking about the Armand family textile business, it is obvious that our knowledge on both scores is already exhausted. He changes the subject.

'That dunderhead has let the water in the samovar run low, there will be no second cup until he returns.'

'One wonders if he ever had a formal education or ever had to do real work to earn his livelihood. His English is limited, and he speaks Russian so fast I can only converse with him at the most basic level. Does he speak German?' I muse.

'Why do you ask?'

'I thought I heard him talking German to Mr Bobrov. I used to work in Japan for Abenheim Brothers, the German trading house. I picked up knowledge of the language there, enough to hold a decent conversation, but that was five years ago. I don't want to be heard speaking it because of the war, people could think I'm on the enemy side, but it might be more effective than English with him.'

'Very optimistic, I doubt any language is effective. He delivered a note to me earlier today, an invitation to a reception in the library tomorrow at noon. No details of course, I have no idea who might be hosting it. Will you be there?'

'I must check whether I have received a similar invitation,' I reply. 'I'm returning to my compartment now and will look on the desk, he leaves everything for me there. Good night.'

So, I'm not alone in meeting Leslie at noon. I had assumed it would be private, just the two of us. He must be part of Bertram's circle. They are planning to channel precious goods looted from Russian nobility and museums through the black market to wealthy buyers and unscrupulous auction houses. The Brigadier must be involved in this too, his presence in Vladivostok is perfect for arranging the transit of precious goods through the port to destinations worldwide. How stupid I've been. All my work recording port activity, all the data handed over to the Brigadier will be used by a criminal gang when I believed it to be helping the war effort. I will not be part of this scheming. I feel sure that is their game. At the meeting in ten hours' time, they will ask me to join their ranks to access the contacts I made working for Abenheim Brothers. They want to broaden their outlets, they do not care where in the world the stolen goods end up, London, New York, Tokyo, Paris, Berlin, Rome, Istanbul, as long as they offload them and get paid. I'll listen to how big my cut will be for helping them but whatever the figure is my answer will be 'No'. How could I live with myself, how could I look Granny Smith in the eye again if I get rich by trafficking the patrimony of this troubled land? Her heart would stop if she learned that her Pip is breaking the eighth commandment or any of the other nine for that matter. I should sleep better now that I've understood how Leslie operates.

I shall go to the meeting ten minutes early, sit quietly and watch whatever comings and goings there are to observe from behind my book. A chair facing the long mirror will give me a view on the whole carriage, its bookshelves, armchairs, tables and reading lamps, despite having my back towards them. More importantly I can see both ends of the carriage, nobody can enter it without me knowing. Vigorous exercise this morning has left me feeling ready for anything, I do not plan to be confrontational in the meeting but will nevertheless stand firm against any form of persuasion. I refuse to be involved in illegal activities. I will not join a gang plotting to plunder national treasures.

Leslie arrives a few minutes after I take up my position. He stands behind me with his hand resting on the back of my chair. We stare in silence at each other looking into the mirror as if posing for a studio photograph. I suppress the questions I formulated throughout the night and wait for him to speak but he simply taps me on the shoulder and turns to rearrange four or five chairs along the perimeter. Interpreting his silence is impossible, the frosted lens in his spectacles makes it difficult to read his eyes, although seen in the mirror his good eye seems to be ablaze with excitement.

Bertram enters just before noon. He is accompanied by his brother. They stick together like mating rattlesnakes, neither Leslie nor I make a move to talk to them. I believe it is time to start the meeting, but Leslie is not in a hurry to explain why we are assembled. This could be a short gathering, cut even shorter when they hear I'm not interested in their plan whatever the financial rewards might be. I must make it clear that my objections are on moral grounds, nobody should leave here thinking I have no appetite for an adventure. Leslie leaves the carriage without any explanation, and when he returns to the room he is followed by Valentina, Yelena and Florentina. This is beginning to look like one of my mother's charity tea parties but with sinister undertones. Is everybody here already involved in Leslie's scheme? Am I the only new recruit? Where is Vladimir Bobrov?

The three ladies take seats that have been pushed to the side in a row, I swing my chair around to face the centre, Bertram and his brother perch on reading tables each with one leg swinging and one foot firmly on the floor. The six of us are now settled more or less comfortably in a crescent formation facing Leslie. I feel a sense of anticipation that doesn't appear to be widely shared. What do they imagine they are doing here? What am I doing here?

'Thank you for being prompt. You all know me well – this team has worked together before with the exception of Mr Gordon Dickson to whom I offer a special welcome. He joins us for the first time.' Leslie takes one pace towards me as he pronounces my name with uncommon emphasis.

Did I hear the name Gordon Dickson. Has Leslie gone mad? I have spent weeks cultivating a false identity and he destroys my alias with two words, my real name. This must be a prelude to blackmail. He is reeling me in and is about to present me to the syndicate members as his prize catch, the man with knowledge of trading houses in Germany, Japan, China and Britain, the man with knowledge of reliable networks for handling packing cases stuffed with Fabergé eggs, icons, cloisonné boxes, spoons, kovsh, precious jewels, sterling silver and twenty-four carat gold in whatever form.

'We are amongst friends. You are quite safe here, Gordon. Your real name and mine, Clement Leslie Chandler, are now known to everyone else here. I would like the three ladies and two gentlemen to tell you who they are, we will begin with Yelena.'

'My name is Minnie Mitchell. I worked as a seamstress in Birmingham before joining a theatre company in London. Shortly after the turn of the century, I came to Russia from Britain as an assistant wardrobe mistress with a travelling production of *A Midsummer Night's Dream*. A romantic attachment here meant I never returned. Russia has been my home for almost fifteen years, I am now head of wardrobe at the Omsk Drama Theatre.'

'Gordon, I am not Yelena's daughter as you have been led to believe. I am a member of the make-up, hair-styling and wig department at the Omsk Drama Theatre where I work closely with Minnie. I was born in the city of an Italian father and Russian mother, my musical studies ended prematurely when my father died. I still love singing but I am not an actress and will not be appearing on stage in a Chekov play, I misled Mr Bobrov to have fun seeing how quickly the false information would reach you. My father did choose my name, at least that bit you know about me is true. You can continue calling me Florentina,'

'I am attached to the Secret Intelligence Service. My speciality is infiltrating groups of interest. I wish my name were Valentina, it is so much prettier than Bertha. I am also a dual national, Anglo-Russian. By the way, I have never seen auras or told a fortune, but I know Harrogate Royal Baths well having translated their brochure into two foreign languages.'

'Bertram and I are not blood relations. We are lifelong friends and joint founders of a boxing club in Limehouse. We work as bodyguards on special assignments like this one. He's Walter and I'm Frank.'

I have more questions than a Spanish inquisitor. If my assumptions about the aims of this group are correct, then whatever their mission it must have been planned or authorised by the Secret Intelligence Service. I now realise my mistake in thinking this is a criminal gang. These people are under orders to appropriate the precious possessions of the imperial family and arrange secret shipment out of the country for safekeeping abroad, most likely in London. Their orders must come from on high, perhaps as high as King George V himself. If Nicholas and his family were to be given sanctuary in the United Kingdom, public opinion would demand a significant financial contribution from them to cover the costs. Selling a few of their jewelled eggs and fancy tiaras would raise more than enough money to appease the masses. Their trinkets must be brought to safety in London as soon as possible. But that might not be enough to save them. I doubt the philandering Welshman living at Number 10 would even countenance comrade Nicholas bringing his despised German wife and their children to live in Britain, whatever the King might be hoping to achieve for his beleaguered cousin.

Leslie is lecturing us on the importance of total trust, the success of our mission depends on teamwork. Dispensing with false identities is as close as we will get to facing each other naked, stripped of all defences, artificial disguises and with nowhere to hide our secrets. It takes courage and according to him it builds comradeship. It feels like an initiation ceremony but the society I am being initiated into is still a mystery to me. Why is the group embracing me in this way? Why did the Brigadier give me no inkling of what was to come other than saying that soft class had been reserved to facilitate some high-level contacts I would make during the journey? Two cabbage-eared boxers from east London, a pair of ladies from backstage at the theatre in Omsk, a young deserter from the British navy and aurablind Bertha hardly amount to high-level contacts. Vladimir Bobrov might be high level, but he hasn't shown up yet.

'Why have you taken such pains to mislead me? What is the point of these elaborate parts you have all been playing since we left Vladivostok?'

Leslie is explaining that I was recruited hastily, there was too little time to fully check my credentials. It was important for the safety of the mission to give every member here the opportunity to test my compliance with the Brigadier's instructions. Had I let my Hainsworth story slip, gossiped or exchanged information between my fellow travellers or engaged in intimate relationships with any of them then I would have been graded a security risk. The future would have held nothing more exciting for me than a dreary desk job or even dismissal.

'We are no longer play-acting. We will change the course of history,' Leslie spouts with pride.

I pull at a loose thread in his assertions. 'You claim not to have had enough time to research my background and yet the Brigadier knew I had been a woollen manufacturer's apprentice at Acre Mills, he even knew the geography of the area correctly referring to the mill being opposite my father's surgery in Lindley.'

'Facts about your family history are easy to obtain. It was surveillance of your behaviour and the contacts you made over a period of months that was missing. We know about the Chinese woman in your life but other people in your circle ...'

'The Chinese woman as you call her is no longer in my life, so you have one less of my contacts to worry about. I am not a German spy, a Chinese spy or a British spy for that matter.'

'That was never in doubt, we are not asking you about spying let alone trying to turn you into one. We are interested in your resilience, your adaptability, your ability to take on a new identity, your capacity for adventure and loyalty. We also needed to test your political leanings.'

'I am not an activist.'

'We have come to that conclusion already.'

'But I have deep reservations about spiriting treasures out of the country, whatever the outcome of the present situation I believe they belong here.'

'Rumours of such plans are rife, but we have no part in them,' Leslie assures me.

He is behaving like an excitable young pup. I must focus his energies by asserting myself as the only one in this litter with gravitas.

'I remind you that my job is to deliver the diplomatic bag to the British Ambassador in person at our embassy in Petrograd. Anything you have in mind that prevents me from fulfilling that duty is out of the question.'

'I regret you will not have the pleasure of meeting Sir George Buchanan in Petrograd. Any hopes you had of reminiscing with him about Stirlingshire will have to wait.' His reference to the Ambassador's origins and my own is a deliberate demonstration of his superior knowledge, he wants to keep me in my place.

'Don't be ridiculous, Stirlingshire is irrelevant in this context. Sir George has much more important business than me, but I have nothing more important than delivering the bag to him.'

'Let's talk about the bag. Please empty it on the table where everyone can see the contents.'

The Gladstone is on the floor by my side, I create some thinking time by fumbling for the key. I could refuse to comply with Leslie's request but it would achieve nothing, there is no alternative to playing along. A neatly folded flannel union suit lays on top of the other contents, I remove it discreetly having placed it there to indicate any meddling with my affairs. A loosely unscrewed fountain pen buried within the folds of the drop seat flap would leave a tell-tale trail of blue ink on the underwear should anybody interfere with the contents of the bag. The pen has never leaked, nothing has ever been disturbed.

I have opened the bag frequently since leaving Vladivostok to reassure myself that all is in order. There have been times when I had to fight hard against the temptation to peek more closely at the documents inside, but I have won all those battles so far. Now I come close to committing treachery by removing the two ordinary looking envelopes and the bulky diplomatic bag secured by a consular seal. My life is dedicated to their safety, I sacrificed a future with Ling for them and now they lie there exposed and vulnerable like newborn triplets.

'Gordon, please break the seal on the leather wallet and empty the contents,' Leslie asks without any hint of his request being a command.

I refuse, it would be a breach of duty and against all my best instincts. I pledged to deliver this bag intact to the embassy and that is what I intend to do. But as Walter and Frank move slowly towards me I get flashbacks, I feel threatened. The trauma of being attacked in Ping Yao surfaces uncontrollably, this is a repeat of being hounded by violent Boxers. There is nobody to shield me this time, nobody who cares whether I live or die.

I hear Frank offer some threatening assistance.

'Let us help you, these seals can be tricky.'

'You can overpower me and do whatever you want with the bag, but I will not open it voluntarily, I have pledged to guard it with my life,' I reply folding my arms tightly.

Leslie takes control, picks it up, breaks the seal and tips the contents on the desk. He flicks through the papers before showing them to me. Every page is blank.

CHAPTER 7

THE MAJOR GENERAL

Bobrov should have joined the meeting by now. His strange daily rhythm is governed by sleep patterns foreign to me – a spell in bed before lunch instead of a siesta after, followed by a late afternoon nap. The monotony of the day and the numerous changes in time zones could account for this routine but I ascribe it to excess alcohol consumption. Nevertheless, it is surprising that a man whose curiosity is second only to his dandyism would miss an event like this one, perhaps he has overslept. I suspect he has knowledge of the diplomatic bag being stuffed with blank pages although I cannot accuse him of switching the contents without having any proof. Nobody, not even Bobrov, could have done this without leaving a trace. Before we arrived in Irkutsk, Minnie, or Yelena as she was then, let slip that he is a German spy.

'Leslie, what is Vladimir's real name and why is he not at this meeting?'

'Nobody here knows Vladimir's real name. He is not with us because he missed the train when it pulled out of Irkutsk station earlier than scheduled.'

He didn't miss the train, he deliberately failed to board it. He must have raided my bag days ago, replaced the contents of the diplomatic bag with a sheaf of blank papers and by now the confidential British Embassy mail is in the hands of the German spy network. My Heath Robinson contraption employing the fountain pen ink failed miserably, I could face charges, there will be deep suspicions about my true loyalties and anger at my incompetence. My efforts to support my country and its allies in this war are for nothing. Worse than nothing.

A smile broadens on Leslie's face. When the train stopped in Irkutsk for repairs, Vladimir Bobrov decided he would make the most of a night in the city before returning to his carriage the following morning. Leslie made a room reservation for him in a swanky hotel requesting the clerk on the front desk to arrange some night-time company. For a modest fee, a libidinous youth, a handsome lad with experience of attending to clients' special needs could easily be found working the streets. A rent boy for Bobrov, someone to share his bathtub, someone he could wash with perfumed soap, shower with an expensive rare fragrance and transform into the irresistibly sweet-smelling companion of his urgent fantasies. Bobrov's pleasure no doubt heightened by the bouquet of wild berries given off by a lovingly decanted Burgundy wine, appreciated by the connoisseur but nothing more than grape juice to the young man. A juice that guarantees lively action without dampening performance, providing it is consumed in exactly the right quantity. Leslie chuckles through a list of guesses about what happened in that hotel room, the slow disrobing, the whipping, the ardent whimpering. What matters is the boy delivered on all those promises and the most important one of all, he kept Bobrov occupied in bed until the third whistle blew.

'I had to get him off this train, he was a most unwelcome fellow traveller. The German spy in our midst was another reason for the play-acting that has been going on. All soft-class carriages were supposed to be for our exclusive use throughout the entire journey but Bobrov somehow managed to get a reservation, from a corrupt railway clerk no doubt. Now I have dispensed with the German spy we are free to talk openly.'

'There must be another ten or eleven stops before we reach Petrograd. Supposing more travellers join the train, we might get another Bobrov. One we can't get rid of with a rent boy.'

'There is no risk of that happening. Before reaching Novonikolayevsk, I will announce a case of pneumonia in soft class and post quarantine notices on the carriage doors warning others not to enter. That means everyone here must stay on board at all times, no stretching your legs on the platform, no visiting Omsk or other stops along the way.'

'There are still envelopes to open, Gordon. Can you confirm these are the two you collected from the consulate in Vladivostok on the morning you boarded this train?'

The Brigadier and I had signed across the sealed flaps that morning and the consular stamp was added before I set off for the railway station. Of course, these are the envelopes. It might be possible to replicate the consular stamp, but I defy anyone to forge my signature. I have guarded them night and day and have confidence that whatever I pull from them now was there when they were closed. Both envelopes are thin, there can be no more than one or two sheets of paper inside, neither is addressed but they bear the letters A and B. I instinctively open A first. It contains the draft in my name for fourteen thousand roubles that I had expected to find somewhere amongst the papers. In envelope B there is one sheet of paper ruled into five sections. The top section bears the words 'Consular, Russia', the one below it has a six-digit reference number and to the right is a date stamp 'Oct 9 1917'. The two larger sections below, headed 'Subject' and 'Minutes' in red ink, have been completed by typewriter. It appears that an error in the subject, John Gordon Dixon, was corrected hurriedly by hand to Dickson. The minutes, signed by two individuals, are so brief I can digest them in less than thirty seconds.

> The diplomatic bag sealed on 9 Oct 1917 is filled with blank papers
>
> Mr Dickson is requested to co-operate in all matters with the instructions given by Mr Chandler who will countersign this document
>
> The RS 14,000 draft is payment for Mr Dickson's services (additional to RS 4,000 commission paid to him in cash on this date)

The Brigadier's signature on the outside of the envelope matches the one appearing on the minutes. Leslie takes a pen and signs. His signature is identical to the one appended to the minutes before the envelopes were sealed in Vladivostok. This reassures me that the Brigadier and Leslie are collaborators, but where is the proof of intention and proof of Chandler's dependability when all I see is proof of being wilfully misled? If I am not on this train acting as a diplomatic courier, then what the hell is my purpose?

'I can only operate on relationships built on trust. You are not my superior officer, Leslie, there is no evidence of your willingness to work with me as an equal partner and these papers tell me nothing of value except that fourteen thousand roubles are at stake for my cooperation in some scheme that I still know nothing about. I'm going to my compartment to destroy the false correspondence bearing the name Hainsworth, it is now more of a liability than an asset. Gordon Hainsworth is a fiction of the past.'

'Don't do that now, Gordon, those papers could still be useful. We'll talk about that later, there is work to do first. Walter, Frank, Bertha and I will stay here. Minnie, Florentina and Gordon will move to the next carriage.'

The adjoining carriage is a lounge area for ladies only. Two large trunks stand in the far corner, the tables and chairs are strewn with crochet patterns, a half-finished yoke of the type Bertha wears, and a pamphlet entitled 'Comforts for the Men', which on closer inspection is about knitting for the men of the army and navy. A wicker basket holding needles, balls of wool, white cotton, coloured silk tapes, scissors, thread and a tape measure is open at the side of an armchair. A bookmark pokes out from the pages of a volume of poetry, another from the score of a Savoy Opera the title of which is obscured by swatches of fabric. I remove a crochet hook and tatting shuttle abandoned on the seat of a wingback chair before accepting an invitation to sit and take tea with the ladies.

I wish I had been more forceful with Leslie. I should have lost my temper with him, but temper has never had a place in my armoury. It signals a loss of control, a weakness of character and places the adversary at an advantage. I have time on my side, enjoying the company of these two ladies is a welcome break, Leslie can wait.

Minnie reads my thoughts, 'You will never change the world by keeping your temper.'

'I do not want to lose my temper with Leslie, but his self-assurance is irritating. Is it based on more experience than normal in someone of his age or simply chutzpa?'

'Free spirit, the love of adventure, winner takes all. That's Leslie. An acquired taste but you will learn to appreciate him. *Chutzpa*? Do you speak Yiddish, Gordon?'

'Only one word and I've used it already.'

'How disappointing. My grandfather left Germany to settle in Coventry with a small community of Ashkenazim. He was a watchmaker, a gentle man with the most beautiful hands imaginable, he always spoke Yiddish to me.'

'Nobody speaks Yiddish where I come from, I picked the word up working in the foreign concession in Yokohama. You must have inherited your grandfather's dexterity. I imagine your job calls for fine needlework.'

Florentina giggles, a complicity between the two ladies has Minnie chortling too until their musical canon runs out of breath.

'Minnie would never tell you this herself, but I can reveal her secret. Her fine needlework is more akin to sewing up fishing nets. Minnie repairs torn outfits, lets them out or takes them in around the waist, shortens or lengthens legs, adds a sash or a feather, changes buttons, adjusts jackets, modifies shoe straps and alters hat sizes. There are tricks of the trade she would never share with you, but it has more to do with safety pins and padding than needlework.'

'Florentina, you adorable young rascal, forgets to mention that I have never spoiled the magic of the theatre by sloppy work. My tricks might be visible from the wings sometimes but never from the auditorium and although they can be made to work in comic opera, there are no shortcuts in ballet costumes. Close-fitting tunics, bodices decorated with pearls and floral crowns all need detailed handiwork to make and maintain in good condition.'

'Minnie often uses safety pins on the backside of a tramp's pants but never on the front pouch of a dance belt.'

The giggling fit starts again. Florentina parades around the carriage wearing a wig taken from one of the trunks. Her hips swing and her head cocks from side to side like a chorus girl at the City Varieties, she pulls her skirts above her ankles and performs a jig. Minnie encourages her by clapping a lively tempo and just as I join in the wig slips down her forehead and over her eyes.

'There is no cheating with wigs or make-up, the audience will see any mistakes. Unlike Minnie, I can spoil an entire production with little effort. All our wigs are made from horsehair – this one slides easily to one side and falls forwards or backwards when I move my head, because it has not been fitted to the correct size. My job is monitoring the stock, keeping the pieces in shape on wig stands and fitting them to actors' heads. The wigs are supplied by a specialist manufacturer, I create beards and moustaches myself. Most male characters are hopeless at hair styling and stage make-up, I help where needed.'

'Are those trunks full of wigs and costumes?'

'Yes, there are another ten like them in the luggage wagon. We were supposed to tour a production of *Pirates of Penzance* as part of a programme to promote British culture in Siberia. We are returning to our base earlier than expected because the singer in the role of the Major General died unexpectedly and we could not source anybody to replace him. A baritone is waiting to be auditioned in Omsk, a slimmer man so I will have to remodel the costume.'

'A disappointing end to the tour. I am sorry for your loss, *But of that day and hour knoweth no man.*'

'If that is from the New Testament you can keep it to yourself.'

I'm taken aback by Minnie's tart comment. She could be an atheist or non-Christian but whatever her faith, I am reminded never to make assumptions about people. The jolly atmosphere has gone flat and I am at a loss to revive it.

'How does all this fit with Leslie?'

'We provide cover for him. He travels as a member of the ensemble. I was recruited by the SIS years ago when agents were being sought in Omsk, then Florentina was approached on my recommendation but the others in the company have no knowledge of Leslie's true identity. We can communicate with our counterparts in European theatres without arousing any suspicion, there is much of a private nature that can be sewn into costumes that travel from city to city in trunks. Agents can be hired for non-speaking roles without formal auditioning and for backstage duties as and when needed. Leslie takes a minor role, one of the pirates. He sings better than anyone else on stage but gets drowned out by the chorus. We tease him about it.'

'Why is Leslie now playing the part of attendant on this train, couldn't he still travel as one of your cast?'

'Our task was to get Leslie safely on his way back to Vladivostok one month ago. We had no idea he would be with us on this return journey acting as a carriage attendant but obviously it gives him much more authority. He is now in full control of all the soft-class wagons, as a pirate he would be all at sea.'

'Please excuse Minnie's awful sense of humour.'

When another round of chuckling dies down, Minnie speaks.

'This journey is all too boring. I will liven it up. It will need your cooperation, Gordon.'

'You can count on me, it's about time we had some fun.'

'You will dress as the Major General, the costume is in the trunk. I can take in the jacket and waist in less than an hour, the inside leg should be about right, the sash might need shortening by an inch or so, the medals will be fine and Florentina can do something with your hair and beard. We shall get everyone around the piano this evening for a sing-song.'

'What about the boots, Minnie? What about Gordon learning the lyrics for the Major General's song?'

'There is a pair of George's boots in the trunk, they will be a size too big but we can use pads if necessary. We can't ask Gordon to sing solo, it would take hours of rehearsal. We shall sing along together and raise a glass or two of vodka to the memory of our dearly departed Major General. The general is dead, long live the general.'

'I love the idea, what will the ladies wear?'

'The other costumes are in the luggage wagon which means we cannot dress up, but the two sable coats are here. They are valuable pieces originally given to leading ladies by Tsar Alexander II in appreciation of their artistic merit and now part of the theatre wardrobe. They are never allowed out of our sight so let's wear them tonight. A gala evening on the Great Siberian.'

As Minnie takes the Major General's uniform out of the trunk I am taken aback by the quality. I was expecting a flea-bitten, creased jacket with a pair of plain black trousers but the costume is an accurate replica of what I guess to be the uniform of the Royal Scots Greys. On closer examination the trousers are not black but dark blue, embellished with gold side seams, the scarlet tunic has an upright collar with badges attached, gold shoulder cords, dark facings and plaited gold braid on the lower arms. I have a habit of checking material by rubbing a small area between my thumb and middle finger – the jacket feels like doeskin, dense and smooth but not thick. Anyone would look splendid in such attire. Florentina opens a drawer in the trunk and removes a waistbelt, a broad pale-blue silk sash, a pair of white gloves, a brooch bar of medals and a clutch of drooping swan feather plumes.

'Those can wait, Florentina, I need Gordon's measurements first. Chest, waist, inside leg and crooked arm will suffice.'

Florentina slips her tape measure confidently around my torso and waist but there is a fleeting sign of embarrassment when Minnie calls for the inside leg. I take one end of the tape and tuck it where Florentina was too frightened to go, she pulls it tight to the floor and looks up at me with a knowing glance. I know the measurement anyway. Minnie makes a tuck in the back of the tunic, takes two inches off the waistband and adds about one to the leg and sleeve lengths. My predecessor was not as tubby as I imagined. When the adjustments have been made, Florentina trims my hair, moves the parting down a little to the left and waxes my three-week old moustache to make it sit tidily into the contours of my beard which is made more striking by the addition of golden highlights. Having two ladies fussing around attending to my appearance has never happened to me before, it must feel like this backstage before the curtain rises with the added thrill of the orchestra tuning up and the auditorium filling with noisy theatregoers. I wish we could all be in costume for this impromptu evening but that would mean rummaging through those other chests stacked up in a faraway wagon. I'm having trouble fitting the belt. The clasp is a disc designed to interlock in a circlet, Minnie tugs at it from behind whilst Florentina coaxes the clasp until it snaps closed. She lingers to attach the pale blue sash across my left shoulder and pin the brooch bar on my chest leaving the scent of Lily of the Valley hanging there along with the medals.

'This silk sash looks babyish. Do you have something a bit less nursery blue?'

'Don't be ridiculous, Gordon, it matches your eyes and besides, the colour blue denotes the patron saint of Russia.'

'I know. St Andrew is also the patron saint of Scotland.'

'Singers and maidens too,' Florentina adds.

'Well, in that case you both need to venerate him fast. Especially you, Gordon. I expect you to sing heartily tonight. You will look the perfect Major General when you get those plumes on your head.'

CHAPTER 8

SHOW TIME

I carry my hat for fear of knocking it off as we walk through the icy cold vestibule to the music room. Florentina hurries back to collect a fake sapphire ring she forgot to put on my finger, a detail that might be important on stage but surely not here?

'Every detail matters, Gordon.'

'For goodness' sake, Florentina, the poor man has only one thing left without medals or rings hanging on it. Leave him alone.'

'Not until I find the dress sword. He must have a sword.'

Minnie's insistence on wearing the bulky sable coat to play the piano means a minor adjustment to the stool is required before her feet reach the pedals and her fingers touch the keyboard. Her playing is as lively as her wit, unrefined but fun. She must have had some musical training in her youth, but not enough to carry her much further than mastering tunes from operettas, before realising that work as a seamstress would provide a more reliable income. The musical evening was her idea, her desire to honour the sudden passing of someone she knew as a leading man both on and off-stage. I can understand why the SIS would recruit such a person, she seems familiar but reveals little of herself and on reflection is a stranger.

Florentina hands me the lyrics to the Major General's song hoping we shall have time to practice it before the others appear. I'm embarrassed to get tongue-tied so quickly. Minnie plays it over and over again from the beginning but gives up when I repeatedly fail to progress beyond *equations both the simple and quadratical.* She is happy to stop playing and start drinking. Florentina fusses about the sword, it turns out that her anxiety is less about the completeness of the uniform than the value of the sword itself which is on loan from a collector in Omsk. There will be a large bill to pay if it has been lost. Minnie is indifferent to Florentina's worries, refuses to help us look for it and tends to her glass instead. She says she has seen Florentina in a tizzy many times before, it never lasts long. The sword, its scabbard and the sword knot were last seen leaning against one of the trunks in the ladies' lounge area, somebody must have moved them.

Florentina is wearing the other sable coat, the more close-fitting and magnificent of the two, and an oversized pirate wig obviously designed for a man's head. Her attempt to arrange the long pigtails ends up displacing the bandana, repositioning the bandana displaces the eyepatch, repositioning the eyepatch displaces the beads threaded around the pigtails and so the cycle continues. She could go to the library and fix the wig properly in front of the full-length mirror but instead she blindly relies on her fingertips. A final tug on the hairpiece satisfies her that it is positioned correctly, and she adopts a saucy contrapposto pose to emphasise how ridiculous she looks in the luxurious fur coat, matted wig and red kerchief. Exactly the effect she was seeking, it seems a rare opportunity for Florentina to play the clown. She is corralled by Minnie's constant presence, Leslie is too preoccupied by his work to notice her charms and the bruiser boys' main interest is getting back to the East End boxing ring to smash up some more noses. I should make a bigger effort to be friendly towards her now that our true identities are known. The charade of Gordon Hainsworth has been constraining, I will not let the Major General spoil my amusement this evening.

I fear the others will arrive without having made any attempt to change their everyday appearances – no face make-up, no fancy dress, no pirates to keep me company. I had hoped we would all live the illusion of performing on stage to an imaginary audience, but I'm resigned to the evening being dampened by those who spurn the chance to dress up and make fools of themselves. Florentina hovers near the vestibule, as shifty and alert as a burglar. Her co-conspirator sits with both hands poised to wallop the piano keys as vigorously as the Huddersfield Town Hall organist. When Florentina gives the sign, something approximating to Mendelssohn's 'Wedding March' reverberates around the carriage. Walter and Frank emerge hand in hand with their floating white veils weighed down by crocheted skullcaps and a rich carmine is smeared across their bruised lips. Bertha carries a handmade bouquet of crepe paper flowers pressed demurely against her body. The heavily embroidered black silk stockings wrapped around her boater in place of the missing

grosgrain ribbon fall over her eyes and cause an unre-
hearsed trip forward into Frank's back. Her walking
stick saves her from a fall. Leslie arrives wearing a
roughly made dog collar attached to his black smock,
his hands clasped reverentially behind his back. Laughter drowns out the piano. Florentina screams with joy
as Leslie swings the dress sword from behind his back
and brandishes it above his head.

As the laughter subsides the ladies propose charades. The men are reluctant until Minnie suggests
awarding a prize – a shot of vodka for every member of
the losing team, not at the end of the game but at the end
of each round. Frank and Walter try to wriggle out of
playing but Florentina persuades them to make up a team
of four with Leslie and me. The three ladies will play together in the opposing team. A battle of the sexes. There
is consistently awful pantomiming by the men who fail to
guess a single syllable correctly, and our ineptness earns
each member of the losing team five consecutive shots of
vodka. Minnie calls a halt to the game, refills her glass and
takes her place at the piano. Her eyes betray a certain
sadness crouching deep within.

'We are here to sing,' she declares.

'Not so fast, let us first raise our glasses to the
memory of our dearly departed Major General. A man of
exceptional comic talent and a true friend. I dedicate this
evening to him, let us start with the Major General's song.'

Leslie's toast has Minnie fighting back a tear. She
composes herself, plays the opening bars, Leslie moves
alongside me, places his hand on my shoulder and together we rattle our way through the tongue-twisting
lyrics.

'Encore, encore!' Florentina shouts.

'With you first,' I reply. 'Then with Bertha, after her with Minnie and finally with the whole company together.'

Florentina stomps the length of the carriage in military style but misses lines when she moves too far away from me to read the printed lyrics. Bertha's voice is stronger and clearer than I expect from such a slight frame, she stays close and hits every word. Minnie runs out of breath before the end.

'We've spent twenty minutes singing the same bloody song and I still don't understand half of it, let's try something else,' pleads Walter.

'Once more altogether,' commands Minnie, 'and then you can sing us some crude rugby songs, I expect Gordon knows a few.'

Walter and Frank sing flat and Minnie's playing becomes erratic. Leslie emerges as the star of the show, he might have been born in North Wales, but his singing voice is from the Valleys. Exhaustion and the effects of alcohol set in. I've found myself sitting next to Bertha who is keen to engage me in conversation.

'I don't much care for these fancy dress parties. I enjoyed making the crepe flowers, handicrafts and gardening are my two favourite pastimes, but dressing up those two men like brides turns the sanctity of marriage into a mockery. Are you married, Gordon?'

'No, every woman I ever liked managed to escape me. I move around too much. No sensible woman would put up with my nomadic life.'

'Well, you look very handsome tonight. If only I were twenty years younger!'

'Or me twenty years older. Have you stayed single, Bertha?'

'Yes, an old maid but not by choice. You cannot have failed to notice my hare lip, no man does. They dislike it. I must use a walking stick too, a childhood accident that healed badly. What I told you before about choosing not to have a family is untrue, I would have loved to have children, but it wasn't to be. If you were my son, I'd offer a piece of advice, but I've drunk too much so perhaps I should keep it to myself.'

'We have all drunk too much.'

'Not so, Gordon. Have you been observing Leslie? One shot of vodka to give the impression he is drinking but he hasn't touched his glass again. The man has nerves of steel, he is wise beyond his years and always reaches his ends. Here is the advice I want to give you. Trust him. He will never ask you to take a risk he would be unwilling to face himself. I have seen how you waver in your attitude to him, trying to make up your mind whether he merits your confidence. I can assure you he does.'

'I value your opinion but I'm still waiting for explanations and until he gives them, I will reserve judgement.'

'I expect you will get the explanations later this evening.'

'Do you know what this is all about? Am I the only person here still in the dark or is everybody waiting for Leslie to speak?'

'Everybody is waiting but nobody else is in the dark. Excuse me, I should not have spoken out. The alcohol is talking.'

Bertha confirms my suspicions. I'm alone in trying to comprehend the situation. The group embraces me like a full member, we are having fun together but as far as they are concerned I am still an outsider. When will the time come for admission to the circle? Is Leslie in control of events or is he holding back waiting for orders from on high? They, whoever they are, have me trapped on this train. I might be able to escape from them and their fake quarantine restrictions when the train stops in Omsk, but it is unlikely I can survive for more than a few days afterwards on the little cash I have left. The money draft is nothing more than a worthless piece of paper until I can present it in Petrograd. This conundrum cannot be solved, nothing can be negotiated or resolved, there is nothing for me to accept or reject, I have no leverage, no pressure to exert, my only strategy is patience. Whether I discover his intentions tonight, tomorrow or the day after will not change my life and it will not change the world. I must be stoical. Bertha could say more but she has embarrassed herself by saying too much already and she takes cover from my anger, retracting like a snail. But the anger doesn't come, I thank her for the advice. Trust Leslie.

She is on her final assignment for the intelligence service as the work has become too demanding for a woman of her age. There is nothing for her to return to after retirement except a garden and her handicrafts, but she tells me she worries that the onset of arthritis will rob her of these pleasures. I suspect Bertha's physical impairments have proved increasingly useful in her work. An ageing lady with health problems elicits sympathy, feigned deafness allows earwigging of private conversations in any of the four languages she speaks fluently, frailty arouses no suspicions, but it is a lonely existence. She plans to battle against even more loneliness in the future by offering language lessons to students for a small fee, finding irregular work translating for poets and writers, perhaps applying for a position at the agricultural college in Pavlodar where her brother lives. Her association with the production of *Pirates of Penzance* remains a mystery to me, it must have provided cover for a specific operation she was involved with somewhere between here and Vladivostok.

As nobody can think of another rugby song, Leslie directs us to the library where there is a meagre buffet of sorrel soup, cured fish, pickled vegetables and bread prepared by an illiterate peasant lady who has been sent back to hard class until her services are needed again. The quantity and quality of food deteriorates day by day, but everyone knows we are more fortunate than urban dwellers whose food supplies are rationed or simply not available. Shortages of bread and milk, rising prices and hunger riots are being reported. Our privations are insignificant by comparison. There is wholehearted agreement that the Major General has been honoured appropriately tonight, I feel privileged to have borrowed the costume for the occasion and grateful to Minnie and Florentina for taking the time and trouble to make it fit me properly. Leslie is fulsome in his praise of how enthusiastically I inhabit the character and the admirable effort I have made to sing such a difficult song. More vodka is served to accompany a further round of mutual admiration which is only brought to a halt when Leslie bangs his hand on the table to speak.

'Tomorrow we shall begin work on an urgent and important mission, it will require an exceptional level of dedication and courage from everybody here. The mission cannot go ahead without Gordon's agreement. I invite him to step forward, look in the mirror and tell us what he sees.'

I know what I shall see. It will be the same face that looks back at me from the shaving mirror every morning as I perform my ablutions. But perhaps I'm supposed to see something else reflected in the distance, this could be a trick question to test my powers of observation. Will I spot Bobrov reappearing, hovering in the background to be revealed as a double agent working for our side? I wouldn't be surprised, the rent boy story sounded farfetched. But I spot nothing exceptional, I will play this safe.

'I see the Major General.'

'The uniform is that of Colonel-in-Chief, Second Dragoons,' Leslie replies.

'Isn't that rank an honour accorded to a member of the royal family?'

'Yes, it is. Who do you see now?'

'Dressed like this, with the benefit of half a bottle of vodka and on a dark night, I suppose I bear a passing resemblance to King George V.'

'Nothing like him,' Minnie giggles.

'Well in that case, I look nothing like Nicholas either.'

The room erupts with handclapping, hollering and cries of 'Spitten image'. Leslie gestures for the noise to abate, swings me round with my back to the mirror and fixes the sword to my belt.

'Now there can be no doubt that you are the double of His Imperial Majesty Nicholas II. I apologise unreservedly on behalf of everybody here for the deceit. It is over now. Trust me, Gordon. I had to engineer this moment before asking you a question – your answer will not only determine the course of your life, but it can also change the world. You have acknowledged your uncanny similarity to the deposed Tsar, will you consent to play the role of Nicholas II in public as part of a dangerous plot to release him from captivity in Tobolsk?'

Finally, I understand the machinations of the last few weeks. Now I sense total unity, an embrace into a brotherhood of purpose, at last I feel part of something important.

'Yes, count me in.'

CHAPTER 9

THE GOVERNOR'S HOUSE

I believe I made the right decision yesterday. I must sign up for this adventure whatever the danger otherwise what is the point of my being? The fabric of my life is at stake, this is a chance to thread a vibrant weft through the rigid warp of my upbringing. There comes a time when everything that has gone before finally make sense, the fragments appear together as a whole, there is no more questioning what it all means, destiny takes over.

We sit, facing each other in armchairs and chatting through what is left of the night, drinking tea until a timid dawn breaks late in the morning across the bleak landscape. Leslie talks openly about his wayward youth, his appearance at Winchester Police Court six years ago for stealing a purse, his trial at the quarter sessions in Newington the following year, desertion from the navy and his multiple aliases. His honesty in recounting all the scrapes in his life is disarming. The man has no fear, the boundaries most of us use to regulate our lives have no meaning for him, he crosses them without glancing left or right. This single-minded determination must have persuaded the Brigadier that Leslie could do the job, one he would never have been assigned to without showing empathy for the imperial family's plight. This softer side of his character has been kept hidden. It is only now that I understand his sincere affection for the old Russia where he came to live as a child. At last, I see the whole man, fearless and profound in equal measure, the qualities the Brigadier valued so highly have become apparent to me. Leslie and I will be formidable partners.

Our laughter at his youthful misdeeds subsides as I rise from the chair to exercise my bad leg which is beginning to stiffen. Leslie takes a break to collect some papers and as he returns I quiz him about the Brigadier. It was when the Provisional Government moved the imperial family from the palace in Tsarskoe Selo to Tobolsk two months ago that he turned his mind to plotting. Safety was the official reason for taking them two thousand miles further away from the centre of Petrograd, but the Brigadier feared the former Tsar's position would be even more difficult there if Kerensky's government were to fall. Although he was aware of the imperial family's shortcomings, he thought them a lesser evil than the alternative. In contravention of all official protocols, the Brigadier began thinking about schemes to free them. Unbeknown to me, he had been observing my movements over several days in Vladivostok. Struck by my physical resemblance to Nicholas II, he developed skeleton plots incorporating the Tsar's double, convinced they could be made audacious enough to succeed where other hare-brained schemes would fail. It was reckless behaviour for a man in his position, but a severe reprimand or instant dismissal are now irrelevant. Leslie received a telegram two days ago reporting his death. Terminal cancer had emboldened the Brigadier and in recent weeks he had accelerated the project hoping to save the Tsar's life before his own ended, but it was not to be.

'Military honours at his funeral then?'

'He wasn't a real Brigadier,' Leslie replies. 'I gave him the nickname when he put together this brigade of freaks in which we all now serve.'

Leslie and I are considering alternative plans based on the Brigadier's unfinished work. The one we adopt will be decided later depending on how events unfold, whatever we choose will require coordination with forces loyal to the Tsar. Our intention is to get the family members into the hands of a detachment of Cossacks or the Czechoslovak Legion who can lead them to safety, firstly along little know pathways to monasteries well outside Tobolsk and from there to a seaport, possibly Vladivostok. It remains unsure where they can go from there. Japan is close but an unlikely destination, the Tsar has never forgiven the Japanese for destroying Russia's Baltic fleet back in 1905. Britain has already stalled on its reluctant offer of asylum, the crowned heads of Europe stand like a circle of numb megaliths doing nothing. The Vatican might be looking at a deal, bartering asylum against access for the Roman Catholic Church in Russia but the timescale is likely to be protracted, it is certain to be a long wait before Pope Benedict pronounces on the matter, if ever. The imperial family looks destined for a prolonged period of hiding somewhere in Russia far away from Petrograd or out at sea, before finding a permanent safe haven. That conundrum will be resolved in due time, the immediate task is to release them from captivity.

From the latest intelligence on the situation in Tobolsk, we know the Romanov family is living in spartan conditions on the first floor of the Governor's Mansion, a double-fronted residence with two rows of balconies on the upper floors. The rooms there are spacious enough, but outside exercise is limited to the small garden and yard – areas that are visible from the soldiers' barracks. The captives are guarded by rotations of soldiers from different regiments, reports suggest that those from the fourth regiment are relatively lax and well-disposed to them. Colonel Kobylinsky, the senior officer, and Commissary Pankratov are said to be caring individuals who refuse to make life unnecessarily difficult for their detainees, unlike the revolutionary deputy Nikolsky who arrived in Tobolsk recently. He is a possible cause for concern, Leslie is anxious to learn more about him. If Nikolsky has the power to restrict the family's limited freedom even further, it would complicate the rescue.

Irrespective of which plan is finally chosen, Bertha will leave the train at Tyumen, travel to Tobolsk by paddle steamer ahead of the winter freeze, and infiltrate friendly groups that have access to the Tsar. The servants are not housed with the family, but they go to the mansion for meals. The priest, his deacon and four nuns are also allowed inside to conduct religious services. Bertha is confident that one of them can act as a reliable go-between. The Tsar must be briefed prior to the rescue attempt, he is stubborn and capable of refusing to leave with the rescue party if his wife and children are not taken with him. Provision must also be made for carrying the Tsarevich to safety, his health is so poor there are days when it is too painful for him to walk. It is vital to prepare the family well, the go-between has a key role and a botched operation could lead to unwanted injuries or deaths.

Leslie lays out a sheet of paper on the library desk. We hunch over it to study a rudimentary sketch of the surroundings and layout of the mansion. We mull over the possibility of freeing the Tsar and his children when they are in the yard chopping beech logs for the kitchen stoves, aware that Alexandra Feodorovna will have to be left behind if she happens to be upstairs doing her embroidery or playing bezique. The axes and saws at their disposal could be used as weapons or in self-defence but the idea is quickly dismissed as impossible to implement, snatching them from an enclosed compound patrolled by armed soldiers and in broad daylight is too risky, their lives could end in a frenzy of gunfire. Leslie traces his finger across the roughly drawn map explaining the route taken when they are allowed out to worship in the nearby church. They leave the mansion by a gate leading to the public garden and walk through two lines of soldiers as far as the porch. Friendly townsfolk wait there to see them, wrapped up in shawls against the cold because permission to enter the church is always refused. After matins, and over one hour later, the imperial family returns by the same route. We agree that the marksmen covering the pathway make it impossible to seize them anywhere between the mansion and the church without putting their lives in danger.

Leslie flips the paper over to show me the floor plans of Blagoveschenie church. They are drawn with more precision than the area map. On entering from the porch, the family passes through the narthex to the nave where they remain standing during the Divine Liturgy. If Alexei is in pain his loyal servant, Klementy Nagorny, a sailor with shoulders like an ox, carries him throughout the service or remains next to him on the drop-down seats set against the wall for use by the elderly and the infirm. As is the custom, Holy Communion is given by the priest in front of the Beautiful Gates, behind which lies the sanctuary. I am already familiar with the layout of Orthodox churches and know something of the rituals and services, my landlady Olga made sure of that, but what really interests me are details of the rescue plan. Our agents, wearing religious garments over their atheist beliefs, professional killers without qualms, will attend the previous office. When it ends, they will remain hidden inside the sanctuary until matins is well underway. Nobody in the nave will be aware of their presence although the compliant priest and altar boys will know of the plot, having been sworn to secrecy. One agent will tarry in the narthex, fussing with the candles and venerating an icon, until the family has moved further into the church at which time he will bar the entrance door from inside. Towards the end of the service, before Communion and as the Cherubic Hymn is chanted, the priest will lead the Great Entrance from the north door of the sanctuary into the aisle of the nave. Unconsecrated bread and wine, icons, candles, liturgical fans, the Holy Cross, Gospel Book and censer are carried in slow procession through the nave to the altar. Five of our men, all of them as slight in stature as the altar boys they are replacing, will have joined Leslie in the group before it processes through the candle-lit gloom. Worshippers always bow their heads, touch the hem of the priest's robes and kiss the chalice as the altar party makes its way from the far end of the nave, turns and takes the central aisle back to the east from where it came. The hymn comes to an end with the words *That we may receive the King of All, who comes invisibly up born by the angelic hosts*, the signal for trench knives hidden in the voluminous sleeves of the assassins' garments to be readied. On hearing the final *Alleluia,* the guards will be attacked and silenced for eternity. Leslie will leave his place in the procession to join Nagorny and assist in getting the family into the sanctuary where they will stay until the area outside is secured by Cossacks or Czech soldiers who will then take charge of them.

As I question my role, Leslie scribbles my initials on the floorplan, in the apse. His hand movement quickens as he draws curved arrows, the first leading from the apse, the second emerging from behind the iconostasis through the central gates and into the nave. Then he scrawls a straight arrow facing in the opposite direction, it represents the Great Entrance procession meeting me head on in the central aisle. At the place where the arrow tips touch he overlays a circle with an uneven cross in the middle and stabs his index finger on it several times, declaring this is the exact point where we shall make history. I will be wearing white robes and carrying a candle to illuminate my facial features from below my chin, stigmata will have been applied with make-up on my hairline. This eery apparition of the Tsar, a spectre bearing wounds from a crown of thorns, will mesmerise the guards and with their consternation at its height the attack happens.

Leslie tells me that the Brigadier's plan was inspired by reports of the Virgin appearing to three children in a Portuguese village recently. Leslie and I are sceptical of apparitions but see the advantage of making sure this news from Fatima reaches Tobolsk. Bertha will be responsible for spreading it in the community there, the more the guards hear about it the more gullible they will be when I appear in front of them as the ghostly Tsar. The thought of men being murdered in a holy place should make me queasy but spilling blood is inevitable in whichever plan we adopt. I am waiting to gauge how much blood there will be in the second proposal before passing judgement on this one.

We talk about the Petrograd option. The situation there has worsened further following the dismissal of General Kornilov, the tsarist commander-in-chief of the Russian army. The capital is becoming more dangerous by the day. Rumours of every kind are circulating. The febrile mood magnifies the slightest development. If there were to be sightings of the Tsar on horseback, dressed in regimental uniform, the news would be widely broadcast creating chaos amongst his detractors and rallying his supporters. As soon as reports of his presence in the capital reach the guards in Tobolsk they will question the true identity of the man they are guarding, panic and transfer the family from the Governor's Mansion before having a well thought-out plan. In their confusion a kidnapping operation has a high chance of success and opportunities will arise for a rescue. The ruse to get me dressed up as the Major General gives me confidence that I could easily be mistaken for the Tsar, especially from a distance, but I have some misgivings about being on horseback. I rode often in the Jagger Green valley as a young man, I can handle a horse under normal circumstances but if it bolts under gunfire there is no guarantee I will stay in the saddle for long. Our base will be in one of the buildings attached to the English Church where there are two wings running down each side of an internal courtyard with access fronting onto the English Embankment and Galernaya Street at the rear. I can leave from there and return quickly to take cover in one of numerous spaces off the courtyard or inside the church itself. Leslie wants me to make brief appearances over several days outside St Isaac's Cathedral, at the Alexander Column and the equestrian statue of Peter I, all of them chosen for their historic significance, favourable situation close to wide avenues and proximity to the English Church. Minnie and Florentina will oversee wardrobe and make-up, and Walter and Frank will ride with me as bodyguards, ready to fend off any attackers. These random appearances will each last less than five minutes. If conditions turn ugly, I gallop back to safety, dismount in the courtyard, leave the horse untethered, run to the church hall on the first floor, slip into the niche behind the Brindley & Foster organ, change clothes there and take a seat amongst the pipes with a hammer and pliers pretending to tune them. We christen this the Houdini alternative.

As we dissect the detail of the two options a clear preference for the church in Tobolsk emerges. It has the advantage of keeping our team together, the lines of communication will be shorter, our escape route is better defined, and it is the only location where the whole family is sure to be together when the rescue is staged. If we are forced to make choices there must be a clear list of priorities starting with the Tsar himself and his son, followed by the four Grand Duchesses in no particular order of importance and finally Alexandra. The Tsar may love her dearly, but her German heritage, her dalliance with Rasputin and her damned diamonds do not endear her to us. We aim to save her too but not at any cost.

CHAPTER 10

THE RIVERBOAT

We have been confined to the soft class since Leslie declared a false case of pneumonia days ago, our world has become more cramped as a result but that will change when we disembark in Tyumen tomorrow. Leslie and I will make the journey to Tobolsk with Bertha, the others will return to base, for Minnie and Florentina that means Omsk. Walter and Frank will stay in Moscow to seek new assignments before heading back to London once the war and the money-making opportunities it offers here come to an end.

I started packing my belongings during the night, it could have waited until later but I had an urge to get it done. It reassures me that I am leaving this train soon. My tweed jacket, corduroy trousers, winter coat, hat, gloves, boots, socks, a freshly laundered shirt and a clean set of underwear stay in the wardrobe ready for a change of clothes just before arriving in Tyumen. A few items including the Gordon Hainsworth papers and toiletries will fit in my Gladstone bag. That only leaves two suits, shirts, waistcoats, a cardigan, dressing gown, slippers and a spare pair of boots to put in the trunk, it will remain half-empty even when a drawstring sack containing everything else is thrown in at the last minute.

The Major General's outfit that would have been needed had Petrograd been our destination will be packed with Minnie's affairs, she will return it to the theatre wardrobe in Omsk. When we take the paddle steamer, Bertha will travel as an unmarried woman visiting Tobolsk to commemorate the fortieth day following the death of a beloved aunt, Leslie will pose as a fur trader and I will be Gordon Hainsworth again, a buyer of carved mammoth tusks, sperm whale teeth and moose horns for my father's collection. The boat journey starting on the River Tura from Tyumen is about one hundred and fifty miles, it will seem short compared with the number of days we have been on this train. Like Bertha I am relieved to be changing our mode of transport. Tobolsk is a small, conservative community where our presence could draw unwanted attention, so Leslie and I will stay at a safe house on the edge of town whereas Bertha will lodge with a religious order.

Minnie is hand stitching a white tunic for my apparition in the church. The kimono-type cuffs are designed to allow my right hand to slide up the opposite sleeve where a short-blade knife can be concealed and held ready. She insists on adding a cowl, although I am not planning to pull it over my head, and the tunic will be made a little shorter than ankle length in case I need to run away fast. Florentina is finishing her second attempt at adding scars from the crown of thorns across my forehead. Her first try looked like a string of day-old scabs, now the bloody scratches look brighter than fresh wounds but Florentina says the colour will look perfect inside the poorly lit church. At last she is satisfied with the result and it is my turn to try.

Florentina will not be in Tobolsk to help me, I shall have to whiten my face myself, dress my hair in the style of the Tsar and make up my forehead in the style of Jesus Christ.

The train has just pulled into the last station before Tyumen. Through the narrow gap beneath the window blind I can see Leslie on the platform, he must have jumped down from the luggage wagon the minute the engine stopped, careful not to be seen leaving from a quarantined carriage for fear of causing panic about the spread of pneumonia. Dressed in a peasant tunic belted around the waist, his trousers tucked into his boots, he tugs a soft cap low over his eyes and is parading around like an agitator ready to go out on strike at any moment. Men of a similar mien seek him out, there is a long exchange of what appear to be commonly held views before Leslie moves out of sight. People are attracted to the Great Siberian like iron filings drawn to a magnet, at every stop they swarm close to sell their wares. It is no different this time but there is a larger crowd than usual because the wagon-chapelle is standing in a nearby siding across from the platform. Its arched windows and the bell tower at the end of the skylight signal its purpose as a travelling place of worship for those living near the railway track but far from the nearest church. As the bells start ringing I see local people gathering in front of the open carriage door where a priest stands looking down at the assembly, Leslie must be among them but all the men in the flock look the same from this distance. The priest's robes and a few of the icons hanging beside him glint as the strongest light of the day shines fleetingly through the cloud cover. The congregation disperses slowly as the wagon-chapelle is shunted out of the siding to be hitched to the end of our convoy and dragged up and down this line until the second coming.

A medical report Leslie wrote hastily this morning and delivered to the stationmaster here attests to the patient's full recovery from consumption, pneumonia was a misdiagnosis by an unqualified medical student. Back on board, he waves an official permission to remove the quarantine notices, soft-class passengers will again be free to come and go as they please. As the third whistle sounds, the mastodon resumes the long slog west. Our noisy rejoicing on this leg of the train journey lasts until Bertha waves her arms, calling for silence. She is impatient to hear from Leslie about the mood of the people he has just met.

We listen as Leslie enumerates the hardships being endured by the peasants. Their miseries are fuelled by shortages of almost everything, despair at the numbers leaving the countryside to labour in factories, anguish at the number of young men dying at the front and frustration with tilling the same land their ancestors worked on for generations without ever being able to call it their own. It is only the unwavering attachments to Holy Mother Russia, the Church and the Tsar that bring them a measure of comfort and hope. Leslie also spoke to a band of railway workers, a cocky breed courted by all the political parties seeking support from such an influential group. Everyone knows that the transportation of able-bodied, injured and dead troops, hardware and horses, manufactured goods, grain and raw materials across the vast expanse of this country comes to a halt when the trains stop running. Therein lies real power. The railway workers blocked the tracks to stop General Kornilov's troops from reaching Petrograd and they will be the force behind a multi-party socialist government if such a grouping can ever govern this country. An apparently well-informed character took Leslie aside to tell him that a coup d'état is inevitable before month end, the Provisional Government is finished, Kerensky will flee, Trotsky and Lenin will take power and the war with Germany will end. In other words, the unfinished work of last February's revolution will soon be completed. We debate the likelihood of this happening. It seems plausible although Bertha is alone amongst us in believing that events will unfold that quickly. When she sums up the consequences, her final remark touches me to the core.

'Less blood spilt at the front, more blood spilt in the streets.'

The Petrograd option has just become scarier than ever before. Putting me on horseback to trot around the city dressed in a scarlet jacket now seems like the dumbest of ideas, thank goodness it has been dropped in favour of Tobolsk.

The stopover will be approximately two hours to allow for merchandise to be off-loaded, goods to be taken on for delivery further along the line, and refuelling. Leslie does not want us to be seen leaving the carriage together. Bertha will be the first to go, she will make her way through the crowds on the platform and head to the riverboat station alone. About half an hour later, the other two ladies will leave within five minutes of each other to register at their overnight accommodation close to the railway station. I will step down from the carriage last, move unhurriedly towards the platform signage where Leslie will be hanging around, having changed into his serge suit and greatcoat, and from there I will follow him at a distance to the embarkation point. All the luggage destined for the boat will be handled by a carter under Leslie's instructions. As Minnie and Florentina's bags are not included in these arrangements they are asking Frank for his help to carry them, but he pays scant attention to their needs. Minnie fusses about the weight of the Major General's uniform and, despite repeated pleas, Florentina refuses to carry the plumed hat and sword separately although she knows they cannot fit in a trunk. Frank thumps his fist on the table to stop them whining and finally offers to handle their belongings in return for a handsome payment that no decent person would have the gall to demand for simply carrying luggage across the street. The ladies attempt to negotiate the price and their bickering becomes more strident until Frank loses patience with them and finally refuses to deal with 'two screeching fish wives.' I make the mistake of commenting on his ungentlemanly methods and mercenary attitude.

'I know your type. A spoiled brat from some snooty bloody family that stuffed a silver spoon up your arse before you even drew your first breath. Never 'ad to earn a penny, a rugger poof peddling lies and Bibles every place you go. Home for you was some grand 'ouse with servants, for me it was Barnardo's where there ain't no favours, nobody ever gave me as much as a flamin' farthing. Everyfing I 'ave is from me own elbow grease. I ain't sorry we're parting 'ere, saving a privileged geezer like you from a bullet in yer 'ead in Petrograd? Not sure we'd do it even for a king's ransom. What d'yer fink, Wally?'

'Let it drop, Frank,' he replies.

I plan to ignore him, stepping back from protecting me in Petrograd is no longer topical and ranting about my background with almost no knowledge about it is idiotic. We have only a few more hours together, spending them trading insults will achieve nothing. I should not respond, but restraint fails me.

'So, you decide to speak to me at last. Too bad you have nothing interesting to say. Anyone who claims to be a boxer would have been exercising in the veloroom daily, why have I never seen you there?'

'None of yer bloody business,' he growls.

'Your accent sounds as phoney as hell. That Barnardo's home where you grew up has an address. What is it?'

Walter pulls Frank aside to force an end to this sterile exchange, Bertha leads me to the end of the carriage, turns her back on the men and speaks in a whisper.

'Don't pursue this, Gordon, it will end badly. Frank has a temper. He can turn violent. Don't take it personally.'

'There is something about him that has troubled me for days, I question whether he is with us or against us. He hardly ever speaks. His eyes are consumed by hatred and he seems to dislike me in particular. If he lashes out, I'll hit back.'

'Don't do that, I can explain. Frank had a happy start to life, the boy could count on bread and dripping being ready on the table when he got back from school, his mother always there in her pinny waiting to give him a hug, the kitchen smelling of Sunlight soap, father in his chair smoking, freshly scrubbed after ending his shift. The young lad didn't have a care in the world, you know how it is.'

'I'm not sure I do but go on.'

'Then came the day of the gas explosion. His mother blown away through a hole in the wall, a bent copper coal bucket, fire tongs, the splintered legs of a table and the headless body of his cat all lying there in the rubble of the front room. He relives the scene obsessively, constantly wishing he could have been orphaned when he was just a baby. Being too young to understand would have saved him from longing to have his happy-go-lucky world back again. After his father succumbed to his injuries, Frank spent years living in a Dr Barnado's home before being boarded out at twelve years old with a well-to-do Christian family, a couple with a son about Frank's age. The boys detested each other, the mother spoiled her son and left Frank to fend for himself, her husband took no notice of him, no punishments, no praise, no love, no anything. He ran away the day after his fourteenth birthday to work at a smithy, did well there, joined the Clapton boxing club and by the time he was twenty there were hopes he would make it to the Amateur Boxing Association National Championships. But disaster struck again. A startled horse kicked him on the knee, and the damage has kept him out of the ring since. Walter keeps an eye on him, he asked Frank to join him in setting up their own club, wanted to keep him connected to the boxing world. Please don't raise the stakes. The son in that dreadful foster family was also called Gordon, it doesn't help.'

'I wish I had known this sooner.'

'Just leave him alone. Spend the short time left on the train with Florentina. Don't you realise how much she would like that? You have barely given her the time of day, all she wants is a little warmth in your hawkish gaze, but you look right through her like someone else is on your mind. Am I wrong, Gordon?'

'Not wrong, Bertha, not wrong.'

'Well then, you'll just have to pretend. Do that for me, do it to make her day.'

'I'm sorry, I'm just not in the mood for striking up a new relationship. It hardly seems worthwhile at this point in the journey.'

'Men. Hopeless.'

I take this as my cue to check that nothing has been left in the drawers, wardrobe or bathroom. Closing my luggage feels like a major achievement, Tyumen is the beginning of an adventure that we have reviewed and refined throughout the night, I hope I will be up to the task. The time drags now that I find myself alone in the carriage. Frank has finally accompanied the ladies to their lodging house, Walter is exercising up and down the platform and everyone else has gone their separate ways. The case for saving the Tsar turns over in my mind without any clear resolution, I convince myself that the mission is purely humanitarian then doubts resurface and the whole process starts over again. I should be more honest with myself, this is not about him, it is about me filling a void in my life and seeking a reason for abandoning everything I ever loved.

A door closes with a soft click, not in this carriage, perhaps in the next one. Nobody is expected to board yet. The departure time is still more than an hour away.

It must be an engineer or a member of the cleaning staff making final checks, but the rapid footfall is enough to make me take cover behind the curtains even though they fail to camouflage me completely. There is nothing to hand that would be useful as a weapon, my only defence is surprise, I will have the advantage of seeing the intruder before he spots me. Sensing my presence, the man stops abruptly, turns and looks me in the eye seeking an urgent response to the question that stays muffled until the scarf around his mouth has been unwound. I know the cloudy left lens in his spectacles too well, Leslie drops a bunch of telegrams as he frees himself to speak.

'We are not supposed to meet here.'

'Change of plan,' he replies gathering up the telegrams. 'We don't have much time.'

'I'm ready, everything is packed. Let's get going.'

'You can unpack, we're going to Petrograd. Are you up for it?'

'What the hell for?'

'The river is already frozen in the north – the boat service will not operate again until the spring.'

'We can travel there by troika.'

'Yes, we can travel by troika but by the time we get to Tobolsk the imperial family will be attending all religious services in the Governor's Mansion. Their jaunts to the church are no longer permitted, in future God will visit their house, they will not go to His. Shit, shit and shit again.' Leslie shakes an opened telegram bearing the bad news.

'Shit indeed. That stupid Petrograd plan means I'll be shot dead just before my thirty-eighth birthday.'

'Wrong, you'll be shot dead just after. You will now have the pleasure of celebrating it on this train, a day to remember. Quit the moaning, we must get Minnie, Florentina and their luggage back on board before this train departs. In case you had forgotten, they have the Major General's uniform with them.'

'What about Bertha?'

'She will make her way to Tobolsk overland, we need her there. With tighter rules put in place by that killjoy Nikolsky, Bertha is the only person with a chance of getting close to the imperial family. She is resourceful, I have no doubt she can do it.'

'I can fetch Minnie and Florentina, they left about ten minutes ago with Frank. But after my altercation with him there is no guarantee he will listen to my demands.'

'Where's Walter?'

'Last seen doing jabs, crosses, hooks, bobs and weaves on the platform. He will not stay long. It's freezing out there.'

Without more ado, Leslie dashes off, interrupts Walter's training routine and they both disappear in the direction taken by Frank and the two ladies. I expected the group to return quickly but there is no sign of them yet, if they miss the train I have my pass to freedom. There will be no parading round Petrograd on horseback in fancy dress, Scotland here I come. I'm planning my route there, it will be complex but not impossible, as Frank, Walter and Leslie come into view burdened by luggage. Minnie and Florentina trail behind, stepping cautiously across the frozen ground, heads held low in silence to preserve every last warm cell inside their bodies.

We are barely fifty miles out of Tyumen when Leslie passes vodka around to raise the mood. Everyone preferred the plan that is now dead, we are all gutted by the lost chance to give it our best shot and sceptical that producing a false Tsar in Petrograd can help to save the real one. Coordinating the timings with events in Tobolsk will depend on Bertha, the accuracy of the intelligence she receives on troop movements, escape routes, conditions in the mansion and her ability to get messages to and from the family. Her ability to get messages to and from us too. None of us is confident that such long and unreliable lines of communication will result in success, and nobody is convinced that causing a distraction in the capital will create panic where we want it, hundreds of miles away in Tobolsk. Not a single element in the plan is stamped with a guarantee of certainty, the whole crazy idea must be thought through again before I put my feet in the stirrups. Leslie pours a second round of vodka, he tries to persuade Minnie to play the piano, he prepares for a game of whist and proposes charades, but nobody wants to be entertained, we have not yet finished drinking and lamenting our bad luck.

The three unopened telegrams collected from the stationmaster in Tyumen are lying untouched on the table. Walter relieves his boredom by shuffling them through his fingers like playing cards and discovers that two are for him. After ripping them open he proudly announces that both messages are about an opportunity for him and Frank to start a juicy new assignment immediately on arrival in Moscow. Frank wastes no time leveraging this unexpected news by raising his demands for going as far as Petrograd and acting as my bodyguard there. His ruse is fruitless, Leslie will not discuss the matter until tomorrow afternoon when the emotions of today have subsided. The other telegram is addressed to me.

> *Leaving for Scotland tomorrow to dance with you again. Ling.*

CHAPTER 11

FLORENTINA

It is easy to lose track of dates on this endless journey. I even get confused about my own birthday. It falls in October here in Russia but on November first in my homeland. Conjuring with the thirteen days difference between Julian and Gregorian calendars is getting me nowhere, regardless of the date I have convinced myself that I should be celebrating it in two days' time. It hardly matters, there is nothing to celebrate and nothing to celebrate it with. The food supplies are running low. The piroshki we bought from street vendors will not last another day. The vodka stock is endless, but I would willingly swap a quart of the stuff for one dram of single malt shoogled with a droplet of spring water. Ling's message fills me with joy and consternation, the pantomime programmed for Petrograd is so dangerous there is almost no chance of me making it back to Scotland alive, never mind for Hogmanay. If I wriggle my way out of this commitment and sidle off to Binniehill to meet her there will be a coward label hanging around my neck for all time, I would rather die from a bullet in the head than die of shame. My family has not had news from me for over nine months. I hope they imagine me working diligently in the textile industry, making my way up in the world, respected and influential in the community, living in some foreign city with a name they have difficulty pronouncing. That would make me happier than knowing they have an inkling of today's truth, with worse to come.

We are now less than thirty-six hours away from Petrograd. The group is gathering to discuss detailed plans for our long-anticipated arrival there. As I join the others there are shouts of 'Happy Birthday' and a spontaneous rendition of 'He's A Jolly Good Fellow'. It might be more tuneful had Minnie been given time to sit at the piano and set the right tempo, it is more of a dirge which is in keeping with the times I suppose. Walter joins in the singing but I notice that Frank remains silent, the pair have been bribed to stay on the train as far as Petrograd and participate in the masquerade there. Florentina presents me with a gift for my birthday, an envelope addressed in roundhand with luxuriant flourishes surrounding the first letter of my forename. The date, 19 October 1917, is written in the lower right-hand corner, scrupulously adhering to the local calendar. Her calligraphy and drawing skills are remarkable, she has enclosed a pencil sketch of me on horseback carrying St Andrew's flag with St Isaac's Cathedral in the background, beneath it is written a fancy 'Good Luck'. There is a small lumpy envelope within the bigger one, Florentina joyfully excuses herself for not having an iced cake with candles ready but hopes the sunflower seeds she has been saving up will suffice as a substitute. A smile spreads irrepressibly across her face when I pour the black husks from the envelope into the palm of my hand and ask her to sign her name on the drawing.

'Don't eat them all, Gordon. If you plant a few every year when you get back home, there will be sunflower seeds every November first to remember us by.'

'To remember you by. A beautiful thought but I cannot promise you they will grow in Scotland. The climate is not favourable.'

'If you care for them properly, tend them with love, then I expect you will have your reward.'

Leslie takes out his plan of Petrograd. He has marked key points in the city with a cross and holds his pencil ready to draw arrows indicating our movements, just as he did for the defunct Tobolsk option. Our initial base is indicated at 31 Ofitserskaya Street, which he describes as a huge five-storey apartment building, two miles from the station, where three rooms on different floors have been vacated by sympathisers for our use over a limited period. Walter and Frank will share one of them, Minnie and Florentina another, and Leslie and I will bunk up in the third. The English Church is close by, a brisk ten-minute walk to the north, the Alexander I column is barely a mile and a half away and the other two landmarks of interest to us, St Isaac's Cathedral and the statue of Nicholas I, are even closer. We have no plans to set foot near the British Embassy, located further upstream on the banks of the Neva near the Field of Mars, but Leslie has marked it with a question mark for good measure. I ask him why the Hotel Astoria has been highlighted as strategic.

'It's adjacent to the Nicholas I statue and within spitting distance of the cathedral,' he replies. 'Life in the hotel is unlike life outside, the place is full of foreign correspondents, allied officers and businessmen of every hue who sip champagne cocktails at the bar and eat meals that others can only dream about, pork loin and caviar are rumoured to be on the menu. The importance of the hotel to us is twofold. We have an agent working in the kitchens there and another acting as junior barman, between them we shall be supplied with intelligence, veal cutlets and especially for you, Gordon, a bottle of Speyside single malt. More importantly, the journalists there will be briefed to expect sightings of the Tsar in Petrograd just a few minutes before you make your first appearance.'

'Can I guess where that will be?'

'You can try.'

'At the Nicholas I statue which can be seen from the windows of the Astoria Hotel?'

'Bull's eye.'

'All my eye and Peggy Martin, if you want my opinion.'

'What the hell does that mean?'

'Nonsense. It means nonsense. This whole thing makes no sense.'

'It makes perfect sense. The Astoria will serve as a refuge if things go wrong at the statue.'

Leslie brushes aside any thought that the plan is totally flawed, his optimism is fired by the convenient location of the opulent Astoria Hotel.

If there are no breakdowns or strikes, we shall arrive in Petrograd late afternoon on Friday, 20 October. It will be dark when we leave the station for our digs. I will be carried off the train by Frank and Walter whose calloused hands and over-developed biceps make them credible stretcher-bearers. Florentina and Minnie, wearing white aprons, Red Cross armbands and caps, all run up on her sewing machine, will accompany me on a horse-drawn sledge to the apartment building. A temporary sign, 'British Nursing Home' has been posted outside. When we get to the second floor I will be dumped from the stretcher into a nondescript apartment, the one I will be sharing with Leslie. The following day, Saturday, he and I will walk the city which I know only from street maps. By Tuesday, he hopes to have found a suitable horse. It will be stabled in the courtyard alongside the English Church where I will briefly mount it and trot around in the limited space linking the quay to Galernaya Street in a forlorn effort to form a trusting relationship with the beast. If Bertha signals that conditions are favourable in Tobolsk, my first appearance as the Tsar will be on Wednesday.

Florentina interrupts the discussion to lead me away for a hair and beard trim, both have grown out of shape in the last ten days. I find myself alone with her, captive in the barber's chair where I must stay until she has finished making my whiskers more Tsar-like.

'Are you frightened, Gordon?'

'No, unless you have dastardly plans to slit my throat with that razor blade. I don't believe you would do such a thing, at least not on my birthday.'

'Don't avoid the question, I mean frightened of this Petrograd farce, the one you inaptly codename Houdini. You will never escape alive.'

'I try not to get frightened without good reason.'

'Well, let me give you one. You will be pulled off your horse in no time, some crazy revolutionary will wield his sabre and finish off the work started by the Boxers all those years ago.'

'I suspect it will be a bullet not a blade.'

'The end result will be the same, your blood draining away into the mud and slush of a foreign land.'

'I have committed myself, once there is a beginning an end is inevitable.'

'Don't even begin, don't go through with this. Don't go, Gordon.'

'Too late, Florentina.'

'It's not too late, there is time to make other plans. I will help you.'

'If your plan is travelling back to Tobolsk, knocking on the door of the Governor's Mansion and politely asking the guards to hand over the imperial family, I rate the chance of success as zero, even with your beauty and charm.'

'You might not take this so lightly when the horse rears up and you find yourself lying on a snow-covered Petrograd street looking up at your assassin. That would be stupidity, not glory.'

'To be honest, I'm not looking for glory. I need a cure for boredom.'

'You'd never get bored if you had a woman in your life.'

'I'm not looking for that kind of excitement.'

'Well, you should be. A good-looking gentleman of your age. I'm serious about helping you, I have an idea to get you out of this mess.'

'Really?'

'Don't you want to hear it?'

'I'm sure it would pass the time most agreeably.'

'This apartment building where we will stay is close to the Mariinsky Theatre. I know the wardrobe people there well. There is a three-storey wing attached to the left of the theatre, it houses workshops, rehearsal rooms, an electricity substation and a boiler room. We can get lost in there for days, nobody will ever find us, not even Leslie. Frank and Walter will not bother to look unless someone pays them. I can move about the city without arousing suspicion, bring basic supplies back and at the right time we shall head north, leave this blighted land and make it across to Britain. I have always wanted to see your country.'

'So, we flee the apartment building in the dead of the first night there, disappear into the bowels of the Mariinsky and pop up in London on St Margaret's day?'

'Or Whitby on St Hilda's day.'

'Why Whitby?'

'I was told you were born near there.'

'Your informant has done his job well.'

'Her job.'

Florentina stops clipping, leans back, points the scissors upwards with the comb motionless in her left hand as if weighing the scales of justice. I have seen this pose many times before, it usually signals an utterance of utmost importance.

'Bertha told me.'

'Did she tell you any other trivia?'

'Well, I asked her about your wife.'

'How did she describe her?'

'She said you are unmarried and only wear a wedding ring because the Tsar does.'

I would reply but Florentina orders me to stay silent until she has finished trimming close to my mouth. She swings her head low attempting to look at me directly in the face, buries the comb upside down in the thickness of my moustache and wields the scissors to shorten a few unruly bristles. A triumphant squeal signals a perfect result, she releases the bite on her lower lip.

'Not a drop of blood spilt, Gordon. You live to see another day.'

'Just one?'

'More, if you stop being so duty-minded. If you refuse to elope with me, the best I can do is pray for fog.'

'I suppose fog would delay the appearances, not much point going out there if nobody can see me.'

'That's only part of it. Leslie has a photographer lined up to take photos of you holding a copy of the most recently published *Izvestiya* to prove the Tsar's presence in Petrograd this week. Can you trot and read a newspaper at the same time?'

'I'm counting on every horse being eaten by the starving population before we get there. That will put the kibosh on it.'

'You will come to the Mariinsky with me then?'

'No, Florentina.'

'I think you're afraid of being alone with me in a dark theatre. Perhaps you prefer the company of men, are you missing Mr Bobrov?'

I have no interest in pursuing this conversation, it has suddenly become tedious.

'Thank you for trimming my hair, I have matters to discuss with Leslie.'

Florentina has shown a side of her character that surprises me. Such an unpleasant insinuation about a relationship with Mr Bobrov is at odds with her customary reticence, I ascribe it to the strain of preparing for the week ahead and a doubt begins to surface in my mind. Could her proposal to abandon Leslie and scupper his painstakingly crafted plan be the work of a German spy? Have I been fooled by her impeccable reserve throughout the journey? Do I risk drowning in the depth of her still waters? It is inconceivable that Minnie would have been unaware of Florentina's true loyalties for so long and inconceivable to me that both are German spies. I have only one sure place to turn, Leslie.

'How well do you know Minnie and Florentina?' I ask him.

'Well enough, why?'

'Florentina has just asked if I would skip the horse ride and leave Petrograd with her instead.'

'Has she cooked this up with Minnie?'

'Minnie's name was never mentioned but the two of them seem inseparable.'

'Was this in jest or a serious proposal?'

'We were having a light-hearted conversation, but this was certainly not in jest.'

'Leave it with me, I'll talk to Minnie.'

'Supposing they are both German spies, we will never exit the railway station alive.'

Leslie shrugs off my concerns with a slow-motion shake of his head. My suspicions seem foolish now, the product of a lazy brain. How could such a thought have taken seed? Leslie believes her mention of Mr Bobrov was nothing more than a test of where my proclivities lie. I failed the test. I could have settled her doubts by telling her about Ling.

The veloroom is my refuge. This pedalling machine takes me away from the real world, it tones my body and clears my mind. When this is all over I shall make a new life. I will stop fumbling around in the tall grass looking for something that never comes into view. I will occupy the high ground and survey my options unhampered by the religious claptrap fed to me as a child. 'Good riddance' I repeat to myself at every turn of the pedals as pear-shaped globs of faith-infused sweat shatter against the frame. I am cleansing myself of stale beliefs, I shall be a free man, nobody's devotee, nobody's puppet, nobody's Tsar. I resolve to be Gordon, to go where Gordon himself decides to go. But that can only happen after I get through next week.

Leslie and Minnie are waiting for me as I return from exercising. Minnie is shaken by the impact of her over-ruthless questioning on Florentina, a shy young woman she has known for many years as a trustworthy companion. When pressed for the truth behind her audacious proposal to hide with me in the Mariinsky, Florentina crumpled in remorse, tears flowed as she swore on the Holy Bible it was impromptu and without any German connection. Punctuated by deep sobs and shallow breaths, Florentina confessed to Minnie, 'This is my last chance. I cannot let Gordon die now. I love him.'

I could have spared Florentina this trial had I kept my own counsel, I did not have to share her juvenile plan with Leslie. Was I flirtatious? Did I give her some unintended encouragement? How could I have been so insensitive to her tender feelings for me? I failed to make allowances for the cultural differences between us, her Russo-Italian blood and my Scottish blood have different calorific values. I must make amends.

'You will do no such thing,' Minnie tells me sharply. 'She is hurt, leave her alone.'

'I must apologise.'

'You can start by apologising to me. I knew her reasons, but Leslie insisted on a full-scale interrogation before being satisfied that my female intuition could be trusted. Of course it can be trusted, it's clear she is in love with you, what's wrong with you men? This dear young woman's sweetheart was recruited into the Russian Expeditionary Force only to be gassed by the enemy at Fort de la Pompelle. The Russian High Command, reluctant to send their soldiers to France, had been over-ruled by the Tsar, the very man Florentina is playing a part in trying to save.'

'Why would she help the man who sent her future husband to his death?'

'Her mind is torn. On one hand she blames the Tsar but on the other hand she was taught by her mother to honour the imperial family.'

'This hateful war has its tentacles everywhere.'

'It has killed so many eligible young men, can you blame Florentina for trying to save your life?'

'I cannot blame her for anything, but I cannot reciprocate her feelings for me. I have made promises to another.'

CHAPTER 12

THE REVEREND

I am wearing long johns under my pyjamas, there is a blanket draped over my body and a white sheet will soon be covering me from head to toe. My brief is to play dead which is close to impossible when Frank and Walter tilt the stretcher at what feels like a forty-five-degree angle to manoeuvre me down the carriage steps. I grip the underside of the stretcher for fear of rolling off, releasing it only as I sense the safety of being horizontal again. We progress at a slow pace along the platform, the engine expels a weary hiss of steam, its headlight making the contours of my motionless body clearly visible in the gloom of a vanished afternoon. The noises of people leaving the train fade as everybody distances themselves from my pestiferous form, Minnie and Florentina speak of me in loud voices with the authority typical of senior nursing staff. Their mantra, 'Double pneumonia, highly contagious,' is enough to keep the curious at a distance. The icy blast sweeping over my face is making inroads beneath the covers from where shivers begin to vibrate. I must fight them, I must resist any temptation to stay warm by drawing the blanket closer or shuffling around, any sign of life would spoil the illusion. The rough handling to secure the stretcher on a horse-drawn sledge is a welcome signal of the imminent departure for the apartment block. Leslie mentioned it is two miles away from the station, I can occupy my time calculating roughly how long it will take before we get there. Estimating our speed is difficult without a view of the lampposts or any other fixtures but I reckon it will take us fifteen minutes at the most, twelve if I am in luck and ten at best. Minnie says something inaudible to the driver at the same time as I smell horse dung. I guess she is sitting next to him which means the hand holding mine under the sheet belongs to Florentina. Frank and Walter have already bid us goodbye, they must be on their way from the station to Ofitserskaya Street where we shall meet up again. I have not heard Leslie's voice since leaving the train, I imagine he is organising the transfer of our luggage and making arrangements for the days ahead with his contacts at the Astoria Hotel and elsewhere. The time drags, the temperature has reached a new vicious low, my bad leg has gone dead, and I can see little through this sheet apart from the darkness of a heavy, starless sky. I resort to my old trick of silently reciting from *Hamlet,* it takes my mind off any discomfort like mounting toothache or being dragged through these streets feeling like a naked villain about to be hung, drawn and quartered. Trying to recall the words of the famous soliloquy from the nunnery scene comes in handy as a distraction but today is different, it does not call for such introversion. This feels more like a moment for practical reassurance, *O gentle son, upon the heat and flame of thy distemper sprinkle cool patience.* But the heat and flame in Queen Gertrude's entreaty give me no warmth, I have no choice but cool patience and besides, *O gentle son* rings false. My mother has never said anything of the sort. Perhaps *O that this too too solid flesh would melt, Thaw, and resolve itself into a dew!* will keep me better occupied but the lines that follow have escaped me, my mind is blank as the sledge slows and finally jerks to a halt. The world seems silent here, we must be alone in a deserted side street or courtyard, it feels safe to move, at last I can get my blood circulating with a dash up two flights of steps to the apartment I will share with Leslie. I can leave Hamlet to his tragic destiny and follow mine.

'Please don't move that stretcher.'

The mellifluous voice is unfamiliar to me. I suspect it belongs to a middle-aged Englishman probably educated somewhere near Oxford. Anyone prefacing an order with the word 'please' has not served in the military, the man is cultured, he sounds non-threatening, an academic, a diplomat perhaps. Minnie takes charge.

'Good evening, sir. How may I help?'

'Good evening, Sister,' he replies politely, addressing Minnie as a senior nurse. 'My name is Reverend Burns, of the English Church here in Petrograd. Mr Chandler asked me to meet you.'

'Leslie?'

'Yes, Leslie. I was with him just a few minutes ago. He asked me to say the word 'Houdini' to assure you of my good intentions. I am here to talk with Mr Dickson.'

'Gordon to his friends. He is under that sheet on a thin strip of canvas freezing to death. He must be moved inside first,' Florentina urges.

141

The Reverend is sympathetic to my plight. Much to my relief Frank and Walter carry me upstairs to the apartment, it feels relatively warm as we enter but is probably not much more than sixty degrees given the lack of heating fuel in the city. I resist the urge to fidget, nobody else has slipped out of character either, we are waiting for the Reverend to speak.

'Leslie has briefed me on your plans. I must preface my remarks by telling you that I am not authorised to assist you, my bishop would certainly forbid it were he to be consulted. However, I have decided this matter does not require his prior approval. I can help your cause indirectly through the good offices of Sergey, the church caretaker, who is eager to offer support. He is reliable, speaks good English, he knows every inch of the city and is also a horse whisperer. When you have defrosted, I would very much like to greet you face to face.'

I shake off the white sheet, sit up swathed in the blanket and look around. It feels like a rebirth. All eyes are on me, shocked to see the pallor of my skin and the icy crystals clinging to my eyebrows and beard.

'You have delivered a ghostly Saint Nicholas, not the Nicholas Romanov double I was expecting,' exclaims the Reverend to a humourless Frank.

I reward the expectant onlookers by drawing breath and gaining a rosier hue just like a healthy newborn baby. My first words 'All the world's a stage' give him the cue to a line I am about to quote but he steals it from me.

'And one man in his time plays many parts,' the Reverend adds seamlessly.

'Yes, I must have played three or four in the last month alone, none of which I was auditioned for. Good evening, Reverend Burns, I am delighted to meet you. I appreciate you conveying the caretaker's interest, he is an unexpected addition to our little project.'

'Whatever God sends is acceptable, as the Tsar would say. I hope you feel the same about Sergey.'

'I am grateful for any help offered, Reverend Burns. Right now, I would be grateful for help rising from this stretcher, my bad leg does not function well at this temperature. Where is Leslie?'

'He was on his way to the Fontanka River Embankment and from there to the Astoria to collect food. He should be here within an hour.'

'Why the embankment?'

'He can obtain medical supplies from a military hospital there in case you need them later in the week.'

'You mean when I get slaughtered by the angry crowd.'

'I'm glad you bring up the delicate subject of slaughter. I'm here to talk about arrangements for your funeral.'

Florentina stifles a squeal, the men remain impassive and Minnie occupies herself folding the sheet until it becomes a small, fat, horse-shit stained rectangle. I study the Reverend. His round shoulders and the bags under his eyes camouflage a lively charm that appears to be under threat from the weight of caring for the physical and spiritual needs of the destitute, the lonely and the frightened. He is not a man to allow his own fears to surface, the job is about steering his flock through a gate into the next world with calm confidence. We all need survival kits, his is bluntness.

'We need to kill you first. I am not in the habit of conducting funerals for warm bodies.'

'That's something we can agree on straight away, I have never fancied being buried alive.'

'Excellent! Sergey will be in charge. He is not as enthusiastic about funerals as his predecessor who relished in them, but I can rely on him to do the job well. The man who arrived here by train from Vladivostok and was too sick to walk off it unaided, a case of double pneumonia I believe, must disappear from circulation without trace. His body will be transported from the English Church to Smolenskoe Lutheran Cemetery and buried in Section Three where a small wooden cross will mark the grave. I shall follow the hearse across the Neva to the cemetery on Goloday Island as the sole mourner, having entered your name on the burial register but unaware of who lies in the coffin.'

'Gordon Dickson is dead, long live Gordon Dickson?'

'Yes. I will hold the funeral on Monday or Tuesday latest, it depends on when these two gentlemen can find me a body.'

Frank and Walter suddenly tune in to the conversation. There is an unexpected opportunity to make money.

'Tell us what we need to do,' they chime, not quite in unison.

'There is no shortage of dead bodies on the streets of Petrograd. I suggest you rise early tomorrow morning and look around this district, people die all the time from acts of violence and starvation, they never get to the front of the bread queue or to the morgue. A male body without a bullet in his head is preferable. There is no risk of finding a fat one so that makeshift stretcher should be robust enough for transportation. Carry it to the British Factory block fronting onto the English Embankment, the access is via 57 Galernaya Street. There are two wings running down each side of the courtyard with cavernous storage spaces on the ground floor. Sergey will meet you there.'

'When my identity has disappeared ...'

'Consider it gone already, Gordon. You are now a faceless, stateless non-person until the moment you sit on a horse in uniform. Then you become a Romanov, a deposed Tsar about to reclaim the imperial crown, a brave absconder from captivity, the adored Little Father Tsar still blessed with sacred and divine power.'

'Will you bury Gordon Hainsworth at the same time?'

'I know nothing about him. I have not been booked for a double funeral, please check with Leslie when he arrives. The only other matter is the spelling of your family name. It will be recorded as 'Dixon' in the burial register, which gives me some flexibility to confirm or deny that this burial has a connection with Gordon Dickson. One never knows who might ask.'

'Perfect. I may want my name back one day without digging for it in a Lutheran cemetery.'

'You will need a new identity before leaving Petrograd. Sergey can arrange everything. He has all the necessary contacts to obtain a convincing laissez-passer for you. Have you thought about your new name?'

'Yes, I will be Dr John Dickson, assigned to a British hospital caring for Russian military casualties. An admirable calling that should offer some protection and not attract any unwanted attention. Besides, I own a Gladstone bag with that name seared into the leather for all time, a more credible form of identity than any government paper. I was named John after my father who was named John after his father, Gordon was added in the middle to please my mother. The simplicity of John Dickson appeals to me. All the spies in this country are operating under elaborate false identities, they spend their time spinning lies and trying to uncover the truth, my name will drive them crazy because it hides nothing.'

'Very well, Dr Dickson. I have one final piece of advice for you. Many Tsarist officials have been held prisoner in the Peter and Paul Fortress, although the Tsar himself was never sent there. Do not allow yourself to be captured alive, anyone impersonating him may be a good enough prize for those who want the Tsar back in Petrograd, sitting not on the imperial throne but in a prison cell awaiting execution. As you may know, hospitality in the fortress falls somewhat short of that offered by the Astoria. I wish you well, no doubt we shall meet again.'

Leslie has brought enough meatball soup and rye bread for all. Nobody asks where he procured it, we all know. He has other provisions too, but they stay unwrapped for tomorrow, much to Frank and Walter's disappointment. We eat in silence. Everybody is alone with their thoughts. Minnie and Leslie are inscrutable, Florentina seems consumed by worry, her thoughts and mine are in turmoil probably for the same reasons. I was unaware of the dire conditions in the Peter and Paul

Fortress, but the vicar has set images of a violent, cold, squalid, rat-infested prison scurrying around in my mind. Incarceration with only hunger and loneliness on the menu has become my worst nightmare. I resolve to break this unbearable silence by asking Frank to kill me if he sees me being taken prisoner, but for some reason I cannot ask him in front of Florentina.

'Leslie, what happens to Gordon Hainsworth? Are we killing him off too? The vicar didn't seem to know whether to hold one funeral or two.'

'There is no need for a Hainsworth body, but you must destroy the textile samples and all papers with his name on. Burn them in the stove, the man never existed. Tomorrow I will show you the central landmarks. Wear your ushanka hat with the ear flaps pulled down and wind a scarf over your mouth, only your eyes should be visible. We will walk the streets around St Isaac's Cathedral, and I can also show you the location of the British Embassy, our refuge of last resort. The Trinity Bridge across the Neva is close by, if we walk halfway along it and look back on the city you will get a better idea of its layout.'

'When will we visit the English Church?'

'Members of the regular congregation are always eager to meet new people after the Sunday services end, they would swarm all over you asking questions and marvelling at how much you resemble the Tsar. We will not go there until Monday when the place is quiet.'

'So, tomorrow is the cathedral, the Astoria, the Nicholas I statue, Alexander Column and the embassy?'

'You will be able to see the Peter and Paul Fortress too, it's visible from the bridge.'

CHAPTER 13

THE STALLION

Every time I turn over in bed a new thought wards off sleep. My ancestors are parading through my mind, Ling and Florentina battle in turn for my attention and every landmark I visited with Leslie yesterday appears as my calvary. Petrograd surfaces in my waking dreams like a beautiful woman infected with smallpox, pustules erupting everywhere. Bonfires burn in the streets, hunger has turned the population to looting, violence and despair, everyone wears black, animals lie dead, stripped of edible parts, and blood seeps through the snow drifts from the wounds of those buried beneath. I have never seen anywhere as clarty as this. And yet, all this misery, dirt and bloodshed is playing out against a magnificent backdrop of Russian baroque and neo-classical architecture – the palaces, the churches, squares, broad avenues and bridges, the richness of it all. My mind turns to Bertha who must be in Tobolsk by now. If she is unable to give the go-ahead this week the implementation of our plan will have to be postponed. There could be many more days of waiting. Leslie and I understand that she has been given an almost impossible task. Nobody can approach the imperial family, so how can she know their mental state and the conditions they live in other than from second-hand sources? How accurately can she judge their readiness to be kidnapped by friendly forces when their captors move them out of the Governor's Mansion?

If Reverend Burns agrees I will attend my own funeral as a mourner. It could be a dress rehearsal for the real thing. I need to get out of this room, inhale the icy air, exercise my legs and feel the mood in the city. There was an unhealthy atmosphere in the streets yesterday. I lack perspective on how bad it is relative to recent weeks, but like dams bursting and liners hitting icebergs, disaster lurks, disaster builds but disaster happens unannounced.

When dawn breaks, I will collect all my personal belongings and give them to Leslie with instructions to deliver everything to my father in Huddersfield in the event I do not get through this alive. The most valuable item I own is a pair of two-tone enamel and silver cufflinks. Mr Abenheim gave them as a gift to all his male employees when he received the Imperial Honour from the Japanese Emperor. I would like my namesake Gordon, one of my sister Connie's five children, to inherit them when he reaches twenty-one. She must have given birth to her sixth child by now, according to my father's most recent letter the baby was due last March. I replied to him by return but there has been no news from home since then. I also own that useless watch with the time stuck at six o'clock, a rump of roubles, an albert chain, tie pin and the Gladstone bag itself but none of these have much value. At the rate this country is declining the roubles will soon be worthless, life has been battered out of the bag and neither the chain nor the pin would give the slightest reading on a jeweller's balance. I have written a short letter to my family. Finding the words was difficult, I cannot explain the why and the wherefore, and I cannot recount these covert operations in detail for fear of endangering others. I mention only the joy of a long train journey in stimulating company, my good health and excitement at arriving in this famous city. I will put the letter with the other affairs entrusted to Leslie. My sole enduring legacy is the mystery of what brings me here.

A mug of tea would be welcome but I hesitate to rise from my bed for fear of waking Leslie. I must lie here quietly for another three or four hours, staring into the darkness with a merry-go-round of anxious thoughts turning in my head. The time will pass slowly unless I can find a diversion to bring on sleep. I begin by imagining new colours for this bedroom, something bright to replace the greenish-brown bile, and then let my mind wander to places where I can claim to have been truly happy. After visiting them all, I start recalling the flavours of my favourite food and before long decide to settle for the monotony of rattling across Russia on a slow train. I must have fallen asleep at some point between savouring the thought of wasabi and counting the number of fishplate joints on the railway line between here and Moscow. It was not until Leslie let the door bang on his way to take an early morning piss that I awoke from a refreshing rest. The banality of him using the toilet is a welcome reminder that life goes on, the futility of my fretful night-time thoughts becomes clear as daylight breaks, my mind is calmer now.

As I arrive at the English Church, Reverend Burns is already talking to the concierge about hammering down the coffin lid. Frank and Walter delivered a body a few hours ago after a search that produced the goods, as Frank refers to the frozen remains of a middle-aged drunkard found in one of the streets leading to the railway station. The vicar is delighted with the condition of the corpse, it has no wounds, wears no rings and carries no identification papers, nobody will be out looking for this man. He probably died from drinking too much rough alcohol, eating too little nourishing food and wearing too few warm clothes – the predictable result of extreme poverty. The usual honours are dispensed with, the petrified remains are unceremoniously chucked into a simple pine coffin, unwashed and face down. I am reminded yet again that life for most people in this city is a constant struggle, many are defeated before their time. Leslie and the vicar are signing documents attesting to the identity of the occupant when the first nail is driven into the coffin lid splitting it from head to toe.

'Keep going,' the Reverend orders, 'then fetch a horse blanket to drape over the top, I don't want anyone peering through that rent in the lid.'

Sergey bashes a few more nails down before dropping his hammer and disappearing into one of the cavernous storage rooms.

'I want this back by mid-afternoon. It has to be dry by this evening.'

'Don't be ridiculous, Sergey. A horse doesn't need a blanket.'

'With all due respect, Reverend, the wind is the problem not the freezing temperature. The only nag I can find is already underfed and coughing, it will take a miracle for it to walk from here to the Nicholas I statue let alone back again. Don't count on it being able to trot. I've hired it for three days from this afternoon.'

'Just get the coffin ready, Leslie can worry about the horse. Be sure those rope handles are fixed securely, if that rickety box disintegrates when it is lifted there will be hell to pay. The dumb undertaker will be here soon. I don't want him poking his nose in our affairs, his job is limited to getting the coffin to the grave without spilling the contents.'

It seems that the vicar, Frank, Walter, Sergey and the undertaker will accompany the coffin, a bigger group than I had been led to believe. The route is by Nikolaevsky Bridge to Vasilyevsky Island and then across the narrow Smolenka River to the Lutheran cemetery on the other side. It will take almost an hour to get there.

'With your permission, Reverend Burns, I would like to join the funeral party.'

'I see no objection,' he replies. 'We should be back here by early afternoon, plenty of time for you to make an acquaintance with your mount before you appear together in public. It is also an opportunity to see where you will be spending eternity should things take a nasty turn later this week. Don't you agree, Leslie?'

'I have no objection either, providing you keep your face covered. Nobody except Sergey and the Reverend Burns should open their mouths to speak until you all return here. That includes the undertaker who will be paid to remain silent. I will be at the Astoria for the remainder of the day and overnight. We will meet here tomorrow with Florentina and Minnie.'

The undertaker arrives late without making an apology, grumbling that the coffin should not have been closed until he had checked on the preparation of the body for burial.

'If you had arrived on time, you could have had that pleasure,' the Reverend replies. 'Sergey has done most of your job, consider yourself lucky there is still work to do and money to be earned. I have completed the official papers for the authorities and the gatekeeper at the cemetery. The relevant entry is number 271 on page 34 of the church register of burials. The cause, double pneumonia, and place of death, the English Nursing Home, have been certified by Dr Leslie Chandler. Sergey has countersigned where necessary, he recognises the deceased as having attended this church as recently as last Sunday. You may consult all these documents if you wish, but I can assure you everything is in order. The poor man had no next of kin and died in poverty, consequently there are no personal effects to hand over to you. On presentation of your account, you will be paid standard funeral expenses amounting to 1,668 roubles, out of which you will pay the cemetery fees.'

'Not even a wedding ring?' the undertaker asks, unable to disguise his disappointment at the lack of a customary little extra. His displeasure is fleeting. The Reverend accidentally drops a paltry sum of roubles on the ground, enough for the grumpy man to signal his disinterest in the accuracy of tedious form filling and start checking the harness and blinkers in readiness for our departure.

A pair of roughly hewn restraining bars are set too far apart on the low-slung sledge to prevent the coffin from banging against them. The scrawny horse, familiar with the route, seems untroubled by the shifting burden but irked by the whole business of pulling yet another load across the city for burial. The undertaker has one hand resting on the point where a wooden arch framing the horse's head attaches the sledge handles to its collar, walking within close range of the animal's spittle as it flies away on the wind. The rest of us hold back, dodging the mushy snow and mud shooting out from beneath the runners, our heads hanging low as if consumed by grief. The grim group advances over the long drawbridge spanning the Bolshaya Neva, as silent and poker-faced as the two stone sphinxes facing each other in front of the Academy of Arts where they wait impassively for the end of time. Progress is slow until the Reverend and Sergey quicken their pace as the cemetery comes into view. They switch places with the undertaker who drops back to walk alongside me for the final stretch to the gatehouse. I will soon discover what lies behind those high perimeter walls, from here I can only see the upper branches of deciduous trees standing naked against the backdrop of a dreary sky.

The brief conversation between the Reverend and the gatekeeper is out of earshot. I expect delays but our waiting time at the entrance is short thanks to the gift of a food parcel Sergey offloads from the sledge. The cemetery is huge, an expanse of low-lying land that looks susceptible to flooding from the nearby river. Immediately after entering there is a track to the left which appears to fracture into numerous small pathways, to the right is a long broad avenue that eventually disappears in a dogleg angle that I suspect leads to another large section of burial plots. The undertaker guides his horse to the right where we pass the graves of an eminent mathematician, a famous architect and other luminaries slumbering below elaborate Lutheran tombstones. Gordon Dixon will not be buried amongst them. His grave has been dug further along on the other side of the path in an undesirable plot under the shadow of the barren perimeter wall, far from the majestic cypress and flaming orange mountain ash. A gravedigger helps Frank, Walter and Sergey to offload the coffin and lower it on short ropes into the shallow waterlogged hole. The Reverend opens his Bible to read from Ecclesiastes, Chapter 3, verses 1 to 8, flicks three pages forward and ends the briefest of funerals by mumbling one of the shortest verses in Chapter 12, verse 7 if I am not mistaken. The last remaining duty is tossing clods of earth in the grave, which both Sergey and the Reverend do with determination before others take their turn. The constant banging against the sledge bars has caused the coffin lid to split open even further, the unconventional position and condition of the body is visible now there is no longer a horse blanket to screen the corpse. The gravediggers pay scant attention, but the undertaker takes an interest in a possible irregularity, doubtless for mercenary reasons. He moves to take a closer look from the graveside but is elbowed away by Frank and Walter. When he finally manoeuvres himself there it is too late, the lid is already covered by soil. My eyes are surprisingly dry as we turn our backs on this subterfuge. It all happened without a hitch for which I am thankful.

The brisk walk back from the cemetery takes less time than the outward journey. After passing the university we reach the bridge over the Neva just as sporadic sunrays target the cathedral on the opposite bank. Its gilded dome rises above the aching city like a shining halo, a good omen for the days ahead until fickle rays of sunlight play tricks. The dome is transformed into a fleeting fire burst.

The courtyard is empty as we arrive back at the English Church. The Reverend fumes that the horse I will be riding has not arrived yet, his profane cursing is not what I expect of a man of the cloth. Without a horse, and with Leslie's absence at the Astoria until tomorrow, the practice for my first appearance is cancelled. The vicar suggests I visit the church instead to familiarise myself with the access route upstairs to the agreed bolthole should I need it. As I arrive in the church hall the weak light from beyond the stained-glass windows casts dapples of faint colours across the floor, the mosaic triptych behind the altar manages a half-hearted sparkle but the organ, set back in an alcove between marble columns, stands resolutely in the shadows. This is where I am supposed to take refuge, feigning to tune the pipes. The idea sounded reasonable when Leslie first floated it, but doubts arise now that I see the organ with my own eyes. There will not be enough time to dismount from my horse, run to the first floor, shed the fancy dress costume for a smock and assume the pose of an organ tuner if angry and violent onlookers are in pursuit. Leslie and I must rethink this element of the plan. I favour disappearing into one of the street-level storage rooms immediately after jumping down from the saddle, there must be dark corners inside where I could hide. As I return to take a closer look at this possibility, the Reverend is standing there surveying the courtyard.

'The horse, if it ever sets foot here, can be stabled in that one,' he says pointing out the huge double door closest to Galernaya Street.

'It looks big enough to house a hippopotamus or two,' I call back to him after swinging open one of the doors.

Inside, I discover cutting and grinding machines, tools, lengths of timber, building supplies, piping, ladders and large wooden crates stacked at random like stalagmites. Towards the back an old tarantass stands on a supporting block awaiting axle repairs. There is enough room to stable four horses. Cover from attack is more plentiful here than it is in the ordered grandeur of the church and there are two escape routes, one via the courtyard to the English Embankment and the other through the window facing the opposite direction. The Reverend joins me, sits astride the corner of a crate and explains that the residential accommodation above us is used by clergy and their guests, a community that is unlikely to take any unwelcome interest in my presence. He waits for me to pass judgement.

'Perfect, but with luck I will not need to hide out here.'

'Why are you putting your life in danger like this?' His tone is more confrontational than dismissive, his shoulders fail to shrug, he thrusts them forward keeping eye contact. The Reverend is seeking a profound answer, he will not be satisfied with anything trite.

'I got sucked in when I wasn't watching. Like so much in my life it was unplanned. One person after another has tweaked my trajectory, starting with my father, then there were others. Some I never even met with names I barely knew, like Governor Yu-Hsien.'

'Governor Who?'

'No matter, it's a long story from a long time ago. I'm simply trying to explain that a succession of chance encounters has blown my life off course, I have strayed away from the future I had envisaged for myself. One person's nudge followed by another, none with any discernible effect at first, have accumulated over time and now I find myself in a world beyond my comprehension. I never expected to be here, I don't understand why I'm doing this, I blame it on inertia, or do I mean destiny? Perhaps I should have put up a fight, refused all offers, packed up and gone home. We can pray together in the hope of finding an explanation, but I fear it will not work. I lost my faith somewhere along the way.'

'I never had any myself,' he replies, releasing the stud on his dog collar.

'You never had faith and yet you are ordained?'

'I'm only a vicar when I need to be. I have never opened The Bible at any book other than Ecclesiastes. I don't report to a bishop, I've yet to meet one. I inhabit the same world as Leslie.'

'What is going on here and why do you care about my reasons for putting my life in danger?'

'Just checking on your motivation, I only work with people I trust. Don't torture yourself with introspection, remember that we are all engaged in a worthwhile pursuit. We are saving the life of a man who had the courage to lessen the risk of bloody confrontation by abdicating rather than marching on Petrograd, an honourable act that earns him and his family a very uncertain future. He is in danger and must be rescued. We might be the ones to do it.'

'But not his wife, she is a traitor to the Russian cause. Why would anyone bother to rescue her?'

'Nonsense. The Tsarina has made mistakes, especially her blind faith in that charlatan Rasputin, but she is not a bad person, she is not a traitor. Like any other devoted mother, she cares for her family with an unshakeable love, you should not believe German propaganda besmirching her. It is designed to undermine the Tsar who was the only person holding this country together against German aggression. But with the imperial family sidelined, mouldering under house arrest with little hope of rescue, only Kerensky's government with the help of the allies can lead Russia to victory. If they fail, the country will be at Germany's mercy.'

'That might be true but given the choice I would save their son and heir before saving her.'

'You don't get a choice. The family comes as an indivisible unit. All or nothing.'

'Well, that will depend on the art of the possible in Tobolsk. Even if we succeed in panicking their captors into relocating them, there is no guarantee of keeping the family together especially if Alexei is unwell.'

'It's pointless trying to predict the timing and severity of his pain attacks.'

'A risk nonetheless.'

'Not a big enough one to prevent us from trying. The Tsarina has lost several close relatives to haemophilia, the rumour-mongers say she transmitted the curse to Alexei and is helpless to ease his suffering. Imagine a mother living under that burden, imagine being consumed by the constant fear that his next boyish accident could cause fatal bleeding. Our concern that he might be unwell on the day is insignificant by comparison. My biggest worry is that she will refuse to be separated from him, her stubbornness will prove counterproductive in a rescue attempt.'

'And the Tsar?'

'Shy and retiring, introverted as the new term would have it, distanced from people he should have kept closer to him. He is too remote from the daily worries of ordinary mortals and too close to those of his wife. She exerts a strong influence over him, the lot of every devoted husband.'

'You blame their predicament on his weakness of character?'

'If you want my opinion, the boy's illness is the root cause of much of the present troubles.'

'You can't blame Alexei, it's not his fault if he was born with haemophilia.'

'I'm not blaming the boy. I'm linking his plight to the parents' plight and their plight to that of the country. I recall the celebrations when he was born, a male heir at last to guarantee the future of the Romanov dynasty. But it was not long before gossip started circulating about haemorrhaging from his navel, then reports trickled out about excruciating pain in his joints, high temperatures, anaemia and long periods in bed not to mention the recent chatter of a sanguineous tumour that appeared in his groin a few years ago. Those in the know say there are long spells when he can't bear to walk. Add it all up, look at how the Romanovs have been affected by his condition over the last thirteen years, nudged off course as you would say. Blown away in a fearsome force twelve hurricane is more like it.'

Clinking on the cobblestones heralds an unexpected arrival. The noise of hooves brings an end to our conversation as my interlocutor jumps up to see what is happening. Walter and Frank are in the courtyard with three splendid horses, I had not expected to see Leslie again until tomorrow, but he is here too. He set about finding an alternative to the short-strided piebald mare that Sergey had thought adequate but could have turned the imperial sighting into a cheap farce. Florentina's Italian network led Leslie to Ciniselli's Circus beside the Fontanka River where horses are stabled, all of them trained or being trained for work in the ring. He met Scipione there who gave him the choice of three animals on the roster of those retired or resting for the next few days. I will be riding an eleven-year-old grey stallion, a complete gentleman according to Scipione, flanked by Walter and Frank on a pair of chestnut geldings both standing at sixteen hands, a fraction shorter than the grey. These beautiful animals lift my spirits, there is now every chance of looking the part on such a handsome horse. He is calm as I walk him around the courtyard, patient and proud as I mount, a true professional with valuable experience performing in front of crowds. He makes me feel better than I have ever been on horseback, the small audience watching these first steps applauds. Walter and Frank have excellent balance but they both need to push their heels down and hold the reins closer to the horse's neck to achieve better control. Neither is receptive to guidance from me, but they listen to Sergey's tips.

'This is looking good, Leslie. I am surprised to see you again today.'

'Everything is going much better than I expected. Ciniselli's Circus is famous but the idea of getting horses from there escaped me despite having digs nearby, then Florentina mentioned her Italian grandfather had worked for Gaetano Ciniselli before he left Milan.'

'Why does that name sound familiar to me?'

The Reverend interrupts. 'You saw him this morning.'

'I don't remember meeting anybody. He must be older than Florentina's grandfather, hasn't he passed away by now?'

'Indeed, he has. You walked by his grave in the cemetery, it's impossible to miss it. A marble bust of the great man surveys all that passes, he looks down from a niche above a decorated stone column. No prizes for guessing the subject decorating it.'

'A horse? I remember seeing that horse.'

'Its head facing in the opposite direction from Gaetano himself. I suppose it represents a parting,' the Reverend replies wistfully.

Leslie is eager to share more news with us, but I stall him in a private moment to ask how the Reverend should be addressed. He laughs and apologies for not informing me earlier for fear the solemnity of the burial would have been compromised, it had to be a mockery of believers. His name is James. Regal in his bearing and accent but not in his choice of language which has frequent lapses of decorum. If he remembers the celebrations for Alexei's birth, he must have lived in Russia for many years.

When all are gathered round, Leslie announces the content of Bertha's message sent via the agent he met at the Astoria earlier today. She reports that rumours are rife in Tobolsk about conditions in the mansion, no member of the imperial family has been seen outside the compound, but Alexei was sitting on the roof of a lean-to in the grounds yesterday taking the late autumn sun with his father. It is evident they would not have climbed up there if the boy had been in pain. If Alexei is feeling unwell, Bertha would expect to see the Swiss tutor leaving his lodgings on the ground floor of the mansion to visit Korniloff's house across the road where other members of the imperial suite are living. But there has been no sighting of the tutor, a sure sign that his student is well enough to follow a full programme of studies. Bertha has reluctantly accepted there is no hope of entering the mansion herself, the guards are suspicious of all pretexts, so she will rely on a priest to act as a go-between for messages. Leslie believes the information from Bertha is encouraging enough for us to go ahead this week. He argues that the family is incapable of assessing the true seriousness of its situation, the danger increases insidiously day by day. The time to act is now. James fears that a rushed attempt risks failure, especially if the Tsarina is not fully briefed and fully committed to the plan, he pleads for a few more days to achieve some dialogue with her but garners no support, everyone else judges any kind of parley to be impossible. It is agreed to go ahead on Wednesday 25th, using tomorrow to make final preparations. Minnie and Florentina will be on hand to make any necessary adjustments to the uniform, the riders will spend more time with their horses to forge the best possible bonds and Leslie will take direct charge of coded communications with Tobolsk.

Sergey stabled the horses overnight in one of the vast storerooms by the English Church, he is mucking out as I return to have a final fitting with Minnie and Florentina. According to them, I have lost weight since the last time I wore the uniform. The waistband needs taking in and the leg length needs shortening to remove some excess material that could cause discomfort in the tight boots I will be wearing tomorrow. Florentina is ready with the tape measure, it slides easily around my waist to reveal the loss of one inch, but when Minnie calls for the inside leg measurement there is a confused hesitation. This is the second time I save Florentina from having to hold one end of the tape snugly in my groin before pulling the other end downwards to take a reading, I might not be so accommodating if a third occasion arises. I'm awaiting a call for one other essential piece of information, my preference for dressing on the left or the right, but the question fails to cross Minnie's mind, she is more accustomed to working with male ballet dancers who dress in the middle. Florentina implores me to wear a layered silk vest with bulletproof qualities, it is bulkier than I expected and necessitates a minor modification to the scarlet jacket. Minnie sets to work on seams, adds some gold braid, repositions buttons and at my request she fashions a rudimentary holster for a semi-automatic pistol that Leslie insists I carry with me. A Browning 1910, the type that started this bloody war.

We will hold a dress rehearsal within the confines of the courtyard as soon as the uniform is ready. In the meantime James and I review escape plans, settling on Ciniselli's Circus as the preferred refuge. It is further away from the Astoria than the English Church, but I can meld into the hustle and bustle of the place, change costumes and become unrecognisable quickly there. My mount will attract no special attention, it will be one of many horses on site. There is also the advantage of being within a short distance of the digs Leslie rents two blocks away on the same bank of the Fontanka, I could head there on foot from the circus if necessary. Having access to his rooms where nobody would think of searching for me is reassuring. We decide that I will leave from the church as planned but only return here if the roads leading to the circus are blocked by agitators or hooligans. The British Embassy is the least attractive option but in the event of extreme danger it could be the safest refuge in the city, one disadvantage is the need to carry genuine identity papers on my person to be sure of gaining embassy protection. Another disadvantage would be explaining my reasons for being in Petrograd, an unauthorised mission gone wrong is unlikely to elicit much sympathy from junior diplomats and even less from the Ambassador himself who is known to be close to the Tsar. His fury at the risks inherent in our plan is a more likely response than praise for our ingenuity.

Leslie joins the conversation as James and I are about to agree on the hierarchy of the various options we have just discussed. He brings news that Russian military cadets are still on duty outside the British

Embassy, they have been there since last Sunday to protect it. Their presence means there is no hope of entering in an emergency, we must strike this long-stop option from our list. He had already thought of his own rented rooms as a possibility, deliberately staying away from them since we arrived in Petrograd to avoid establishing traceable links between us. His discipline has been strict until now, we leave the room at Ofitserskaya Street at different times, never return there together, Leslie did not attend my funeral, he spends most of his time at the Astoria and only talks about our business outside in private. When he reviews the timings for tomorrow, we agree on a ten o'clock group rendezvous here at the church for a noon appearance at the Nicholas I statue where press photographers will have been briefed for an unspecified but important event. I will ride from the English Church covered in a plain cloak before shedding it in front of the Polovtsev Mansion situated on the right immediately before entering St Isaac's Square. Minnie and Florentina will be waiting there under the wrought-iron porch to take the cloak and hand me a tight-fitting, black wool Hussar hat with a red felt point draped over the right-hand side, gold trim and a horsehair plume. This is a significant upgrade from the Major General's tired hat with its wilting grey swan feathers, good enough for an amateur dramatic production but not for the Tsar. The Hussar hat is compact enough to leave my face uncovered. It has been voted the right choice by everyone except James who claims it would never be worn with this jacket, but Leslie overrules him. By the time anyone questions the mismatch our job will have been done, and besides everyone knows the Tsar no longer has access to a wardrobe of coordinated uniforms.

Flanked by Frank and Walter in Cossack costumes, I will emerge in public to the sound of bells ringing from St Isaac's Cathedral, three minutes later we will make haste towards the circus to disrobe as fast as possible. News of the Tsar's appearance should spread fast, a mixture of elation and consternation will be powerful enough to destabilise his guards and mobilise his supporters. I know we could be fooling ourselves, but the camaraderie and Leslie's unshakeable boldness give me the confidence that we have a better than evens chance of pulling this off. I start to think I will look magnificent riding this superb stallion tomorrow and then recall how Granny Smith would scold me gently whenever I showed any sign of swagger, 'Don't you get too pleased with yourself, Little Pip. Pride comes before a fall.'

Sergey returns from an errand waving his arms and forming breathless phrases that make no sense.

'The bridges, the bridges,' he splutters.

'Slow down, draw breath and start again,' James tells him.

'The bridges over the Neva have been raised, nobody can cross. The shops and schools have all been closed, something is going on.'

Leslie is always calm whenever the unexpected happens. 'We do not need to cross the Neva tomorrow or any other day. The burial was the only part of the plan taking place on the other side of the river, calm down.'

'But that's not all,' Sergey has more to tell. 'The government has closed the Bolshevik press, damaged the print beds and destroyed freshly printed copies of today's newspaper.'

'If there are no newspapers tomorrow we shall have to rethink the idea of you being photographed with one in front of the statue. Have you tested rolling up a copy of *Izvestiya* and sliding it down your boot ready to pull out for the photographers?' Leslie asks.

'Yes, Minnie has cut short a trouser leg to give more space around the calf. I can get a few pages tucked down there but I only need to show the masthead, headline and publication date. I will not carry the full newspaper, just the front page.'

'These Bolsheviks are resourceful, I feel sure there will be some kind of bulletin published tomorrow, it will be enough for our purposes. Do you bring us any good news, Sergey?'

'There are reports of unusual troop movements in the direction of the Winter Palace, it looks like the government is reinforcing protection around itself.'

'That should not trouble us, with the British Embassy off the menu we have no reason to go near the Winter Palace. It might be unexpectedly positive news, the activity over there will serve as a magnet for the riff-raff we have no interest in attracting to see our show. Curtain up in less than twenty-four hours, good luck everyone.'

The group splits up on the back of Leslie's sense of optimism and before James can dampen the atmosphere with one of his negative remarks I decide to take a detour back to my nearby digs deliberately leaving the courtyard in the wrong direction to walk alone along the banks of the Neva as far as the Fontanka River, turn right, walk to the Kryukov Canal and then turn right again. Being close to water usually calms my mind, here it is having the opposite effect, I cannot fathom anything I see happening around me. Sergey reported that the bridges were closed by the government but now the pro-Soviets seem to be in control and keeping them open. The shops, having shut this morning, are trading again, restaurants are open for folk who can afford to eat in them, and the guards remain on duty outside the British Embassy. The sporadic gunfire of the last few days has subsided, even though armed groups are roaming around I do not sense any imminent danger or a need to quicken my pace. I prolong my walk by crossing every bridge from one embankment to the other along both the river and the canal, there are so many that I lose count. The truth is, I do not want to count. I feel like a young boy enjoying the fun of a new game where there is no winner or loser, weaving across the waterways at every opportunity and marvelling at the beauty of this ragamuffin city. I spot the circus, a stone building with a huge dome, more like an opera house than the canvas big top of my imagination. As the Mariinsky Theatre comes into view, my thoughts turn to Florentina and her proposal to escape there together. Too late now.

I could turn left and take to my bed, knowing I will not sleep, or walk straight ahead to explore the triangular Novaya Gollandia Island. It is not far but the night air is beginning to chill my bones.

CHAPTER 14

MARY

Leslie knows a lot about this peculiar man-made island. During a long sleepless night on the Great Siberian, he told me stories of its panopticon prison and internal pool, a water tank used for testing prototypes of battleships, cruisers, destroyers and submarines. As I walk further along the embankment hoping to see such marvels my view is blocked by a long row of windowless warehouses backing onto the canal. The prison, an illuminated rotunda without a dome, only comes into view from the second side of the triangle; the third side reveals little that's new until I reach a massive arch linking the dark waters of the Moyka River to the testing pool beyond. Disappointed that the island is determined to keep its secrets from me, I retrace my steps to the junction with Ofitserskaya Street and retire to my room. It is unusual for me to turn in so early, everything about these last few days has left me wondering whether there is such a state as 'normal'. When the world is at peace can it be called normal? Is the inevitability of conflict normal? Is my life normal today having been abnormal until now? I am beginning to think that normal is a concept to be dispensed with when a boom loud enough to frighten the German flag off the face of the waters wrenches me from a drowsy state.

'What the hell was that?' I shout at Leslie before realising it is only quarter to ten, he has not returned to the apartment yet, for him the evening is still young. It is for me too, but my activities are strictly limited because I cannot show my face in public until tomorrow. Leaving my bed to look out of the window, I am expecting to see the rubble of a collapsed building but there is no sign of anything amiss in the street below. The cloud cover is eerily pierced by a weak beam coming from the direction of the Neva, and watching it for a while, half-thinking it is a supernatural sign, I realise the searchlight at the Peter and Paul Fortress must be switched on. The choice between going out again in the cold night to find out more or returning to a warm bed where I can wait until Leslie brings news is no choice at all.

When I open my eyes to a grey windy morning, a pensive Leslie is dressed and pacing the room warming his hands on a mug of tea. He takes a drink before speaking.

'It looks like we're too late.'

'Shit, have I overslept?'

'No.'

'What then?

'Option two is fast coming undone.'

'What are you talking about?'

'There has been a coup d'état overnight. The Military Revolutionary Committee now controls everything in this city apart from the Winter Palace where the Provisional Government is still holed up, and not for long if I read the runes correctly.'

'Where did you hear about this?'

'I was out until four o'clock this morning. My network reported to me throughout the night. Bridges, railway stations and key positions were coming under the control of pro-Soviets one after the other.'

'Strange, I heard no shooting in the street below.'

'There wasn't any, it's a bear hug not a massacre. There were some injuries at the Winter Palace from artillery fire directed from the fortress across the river, unlucky folk in the hospital wing there got hit. It's unlikely you would hear that from here.'

'But I did hear a loud bang late in the evening.'

'The whole city heard that bang, it was a blank fired from the cruiser *Aurora* anchored on the Neva. People are saying it was the signal to launch a final push against Kerensky's government.'

'Can we still go ahead today?'

'I doubt it. We will all meet as planned in the courtyard at the English Church in a couple of hours. I want to hear what James has to say, let's not take any hasty decisions.'

James must have spent all night in the streets trying to stay abreast of developments, he is dishevelled, his eyelids look heavy and his spider veins are more purple than before. He huddles in conversation with Leslie until the others arrive in the courtyard, each one telling stories of the night. I feel guilty having slept undisturbed for most of it, there is little I can add to the news arriving from all quarters. The chatter falls silent as Leslie calls for James to share the latest updates.

'I received reports earlier this morning about members of the Provisional Government. They are still in the Winter Palace.'

'Which is surrounded by a force of Red Guards.'

'I was about to mention that minor problem,' James replies.

'And those inside the palace who are supposed to be protecting the government are quitting their posts because food supplies have been stopped. Government offices are surrendering to the Bolsheviks, it looks bleak for Kerensky.'

'This is not over yet, Leslie. Kerensky is reported to be on a mission to bring troops from outside the city.'

'He has no hope of succeeding.'

'But if he does get reinforcements, if the stand-off at the barricade outside the palace gets ugly, there will be an almighty bloody confrontation. No telling who comes out on top in that scenario.'

'My hunch is there is no appetite for a full-scale battle, the odds are too heavily stacked against Kerensky and he knows that,' Leslie replies.

Florentina interrupts. 'How much time do we have before a decision must be made?'

'Gordon needs to be dressed within an hour. You and Minnie should leave here fifteen minutes before he does, enough time to be in position at the Polovtsev Mansion when he sheds his cloak and dons his hat there.'

Leslie is still talking as if we will go ahead as planned.

'I will go and attend to the uniform, don't want any creases spoiling the show.'

When Florentina is out of earshot, Leslie lets rip.

'The *Aurora's* guns are trained on the Winter Palace. The crowds are waiting for her to blow it to smithereens and our inimitable Florentina spends her time fretting about a crease. Who will shake that young woman out of her dream state? An empire is crumbling in front of her eyes and all she can see is a piddling crease in a pair of lousy trousers.'

'Fussing over the uniform is her only refuge from panicking about Gordon's safety,' James adds with surprising sensitivity.

'Well, we are all anxious, even Walter and Frank who only get paid if they ride out with Gordon today. Speak of the devil.'

The two boxer boys lead the horses out of the makeshift stable. The sheen on their hooves is brighter than yesterday, and their manes, tails and coats are in top condition. Sergey has groomed them well. I take care of the stallion, walking him around the courtyard affords me a few calming moments away from the bruhaha going on both near and far. James and Leslie are raising their voices in disagreement about the next steps, and the noise from the crowds in the streets outside reaches a new pitch when all I need is a moment of peace away from it all. I have often been sceptical about the chances of success but now persuade myself that history will be made today, this is a turning point, and I will be a part of it. An image of the Tsar returning to regain his capital astride a dazzling mount makes me impatient to see Sergey saddle up Incitatus, his circus name, but the man is nowhere to be seen.

'Where is Sergey?' I ask Leslie.

'Sent on an errand to get the latest intelligence from the Astoria and assess the situation in the streets around there. He should be back here within thirty minutes. A final decision will be made then.'

'Meanwhile?'

'Meanwhile, you join Florentina and Minnie. Get dressed, get into character and you might want to get on your knees to say your prayers.'

For Minnie this is business as usual, just like another performance in a theatrical calendar full of preparations for programme changeovers, but Florentina is having difficulty seeing through her tears to get the job done. The trousers she came here to press are still scrunched up in her tight grip as she wanders around looking for the belt Minnie is waving in the air from afar. My instinct is to quit this scene, I have no appetite for dealing with an emotional Florentina, telling her yet again that I will not flee to the Mariinsky with her. Any distraction from the steps we have planned would destabilise my resolve, I will not let that happen, I must get the two ladies to dress me without delay. It will signal there is no going back.

'Let's get started, there is no time to lose.'

'We're almost ready, strip down to your underwear,' Minnie orders.

She makes the final adjustments to the uniform, sash and medals before I pull up my boots ready to walk out and seek approval from the others. There is everything in this storeroom apart from a full-length mirror, I cannot see how closely I resemble the Tsar.

'Remarkable!' James exclaims as I emerge into the open air.

'Not bad, not bad at all,' Leslie adds. 'Let's not wait for Sergey to arrive before saddling up, I need to see you sitting on this beauty's back before passing final judgement.'

Walter gives me a leg up. When Incitatus is cued to walk around the courtyard a growing affinity to the much-misunderstood man it is my misfortune to resemble deepens yet further. Having such a powerful animal under my control and wearing medals that span halfway across my chest stirs an exaggerated sense of self-importance that I should be capable of resisting, but I find it intoxicating.

'Bloody good, you really look the part.' The words are hardly out of Leslie's mouth when Sergey approaches at speed waving a piece of paper in the air.

'Read this, Leslie, read this.'

He studies the message silently, lets the paper fall as far as his knees and bids me dismount.

'We have missed our chance. Listen, it's hot off the press, barely one hour old.'

> *To the Citizens of Russia!*
>
> *The cause for which the people have struggled – the immediate offer of a democratic peace, the abolition of landlord ownership of land, workers' control over industry, the creation of a Soviet government – this has been assured.*
>
> *Long live the revolution of workers, soldiers and peasants!*
>
> *The Military Revolutionary Committee of the Petrograd Soviet of Workers' and Soldiers' Deputies*
>
> *25 October 1917, 10.00 in the morning*

The die is cast. I see Leslie despondent for the first time since we met all those weeks ago. His taste for adventure unslaked, his plan trashed and worst of all his adopted country in the hands of the revolutionaries with the Tsar and his family at their mercy. The future has closed down on him, the silence becomes unbearable, nobody has the courage to break it except Leslie himself. When he does, the tone is resolutely practical.

'The situation has changed, Gordon cannot be exposed to ridicule or assassination, the plan is dead. This group cannot stay together without a purpose, we must agree on steps for the next twenty-four hours after which we will split. Quitting our temporary accommodation at Ofitserskaya Street no later than tomorrow morning means everyone will be on their own from then. For those who want to leave Petrograd and do not have the necessary travel documents, Sergey will arrange for them to be produced. Let's get an initial idea of plans, starting with Florentina.'

'I don't know, you must give me time to think. Shouldn't Mary be part of this discussion, she is still in there waiting for news. We need to know her plans too.'

This is the first time I hear Mary's name. I had no idea someone else was in the storeroom watching me dress, it is disconcerting to think I was being observed by a stranger and that nobody mentioned her presence before now.

'Who is Mary?' I ask.

Florentina's cheeks redden with confusion. Leslie rescues her by responding to my question before she manages to coax out the words that are still stuck in her throat.

'Mary is a nurse. She is attached to the Scottish Women's Hospitals and should now be on her way home to Edinburgh. We waylaid her, I should say persuaded her to spend a few days with us in case of need.'

'Need?'

'Yes, there was always the possibility that something could go wrong today and you would need urgent medical care. Mary was on hand to provide it.'

'And nobody felt it necessary to introduce us?'

'Frankly, Gordon, nobody wanted to alarm you. There was no point in exaggerating the risk, we just took a precaution, that's all.'

As I open the door and call her name I get an immediate response from somewhere in the far recesses of the storeroom.

'Hello, Gordon. I feel I know you well already. My name is Mary McElhone.'

I cannot see her face yet. These disembodied words are spoken into a void from somewhere in the dark mid-distance. The accent is Scottish, the voice unwavering and sincere. It must have comforted innumerable young soldiers dying in field hospitals far from home, her soft whisper turning that old white lie 'everything is going to be alright' into a longed-for truth. She emerges wearing a grey ankle-length serge skirt, a matching tailored jacket with patch pockets and a three-quarter length cape with one flap tossed over her left shoulder. The dark satin lining, its colour repeated on her collar, tempers the monotony of the uniform. She is carrying a broad-brimmed hat. As I finally see her slim silhouette, upright bearing and bobbed hair an image of my sister Connie comes to mind. I should not make the mistake of underestimating this lassie however fragile she may appear to be. I ask first about her homeland and then I ask about her war. Mary was posted to Serbia within days of walking into the Scottish Women's Hospital headquarters in Charlotte Square to volunteer as a nurse. It was early 1915 when typhus, spread by lice burrowing into the warmest parts of the body, was killing thousands of Serbs. The orderlies combatted the disease by shaving off the soldiers' body hair and burning their uniforms whilst Mary served with other new recruits nursing battlefield casualties and gas gangrene amputees. Undeterred by heartbreaking memories of stench and gore, she returned from leave in Scotland to nurse Serbian soldiers again, this time at the Russian front from where she is now making her way back to Scotland. A group of her companions has already gone ahead, they should be sailing for Newcastle by now.

'I enjoy an adventure, home can wait,' she tells me as Leslie moves closer to break up our conversation.

He shares his plans with us whilst everyone else works out their own response to the fast-moving events. After breaking the news from Petrograd to Bertha, Leslie will report to the British Embassy and resume his job there as an accredited clerk. He over-emphasises how small his digs in the city are so that no desperate soul will dare ask for a bed there. For the rest of us the days ahead are not quite so straightforward, although Frank and Walter seem relaxed thanks to the Moscow assignment which is still open to them. Minnie speaks next, her route out of here is by train to Omsk where she can re-join her beloved theatre wardrobe and colleagues. Nobody challenges her refusal to carry the Major General's uniform in her baggage, we all know it is too heavy and bulky for her to transport alone.

'And the rest of you? Leslie asks.

'If someone helps me with the uniform, I will take it to the Mariinsky and have it stored there. It can be returned to Omsk next time costumes are lent out.'

'I can help you do that,' James replies to Florentina. 'Then I will make my way back to Britain, I have no future here under this crass new regime.'

'Same for me,' I reply, 'I will never return to Vladivostok. Besides, I promised a friend I would be back in Scotland for Christmas or at latest by Hogmanay.'

'It's too late for me to catch up with my nursing unit. I could travel with Gordon and James if they have no objection. I would appreciate company on the journey home.'

'Everybody has a plan except you, Florentina. Will you return to Omsk?'

'No, Leslie. I will not return to Omsk. If they will have me I shall join the party of three leaving for Britain, it has always been my dream to set foot there.'

Florentina is the only one who needs a full set of new papers for entry to a British port. Mary has the necessary documents, James will have the word 'Minister' added to the description in his passport and I need 'Doctor' in mine. Sergey can get all this done within twenty-four hours. It is a minor task for his friendly forger. We can then travel as a medic, a nurse and a Church of Scotland minister, all highly regarded vocations more likely to elicit assistance than hindrance as we make our way home. Florentina thinks she needs a raison d'être that chimes with the rest of the group. Her first idea is anaesthetist, but a basic question from Mary leaves her in embarrassed confusion about the correct answer. She finally settles on a professor of Italian studies responding to an invitation from University College London to lecture on Renaissance culture, a subject much closer to her heart than anaesthesia. Sergey adds a phoney invitation letter from the university to his list of documents required for tomorrow.

My biggest problem is money, I have almost none left and without a credible story to tell the British Embassy will never extend me an emergency loan. I have no hope of earning enough here to pay for my passage back home. The role thrust upon me, the leading part I was persuaded to play and finally made my own has disappeared overnight. Where now? I look around and see everyone else is shaken by the speed of events, disappointed but not as blind as me to the most elementary next steps like obtaining food, a bed and a ticket out of here, none of which I can afford. Tomorrow there is the certainty of being tossed out of my accommodation into the street. Unemployed and penniless I shall soon starve to death. Some desperate soul will scoop me up, rail at my empty pockets, dump me back in the gutter, and leave it to someone else to haul me over to Smolenskoe Cemetery and abandon me there for eternity in the company of a decomposing drunkard called Gordon Dixon. Why should anybody care what happens to me now that I have no further use as the Tsar's double? I have rebuffed Florentina, kept aloof from James and hardly know Mary, and have no idea who will support my financial needs until I get home and beg my family for money to repay them. My pride prevents me from asking anyone for a lump sum, it will be embarrassing enough slowly leeching funds from my travel companions to cover one expense after another. Ling is the only person I could ask for help, but I don't know where she is now, my best guess is somewhere between China and Scotland.

Leslie is unaware of my financial plight. He seems content, in a strangely paternalistic way given his young years, that everyone has taken responsibility for whatever the immediate future holds for them. We can all let down our guard now. When I shave off my beard tonight I shall feel like a free man released from an indenture with only a moustache to remind me of my commitment to save the Tsar. My bizarre bond with Leslie will doubtless unravel within days, we have little left in common except saying some unavoidably awkward farewell no later than tomorrow morning. He is a survivor. I expect we will part with only a simple handshake and unspoken regret. Like a chameleon he will blend in wherever and whenever his safety depends on adopting a low profile, with his sharp brain at work behind a new alias and an unremarkable facade. Leslie can easily go to ground, adopting a British or Russian identity whichever serves him best, an option beyond the reach of those of us with uniquely British backgrounds. We cannot switch at will. Our spoken Russian comes with an indelible accent typical of most foreigners who only start to learn the language as adults, and our cultural adaptation is incomplete with lapses in basic knowledge of Russian life. None of this will matter too much if we get out of here before the new leadership and their followers decide to foster anti-British attitudes, unlike Leslie none of us can credibly pretend to be Russian. We must leave this country sooner rather than later.

Mary rejoices at how well she slept on the floor in Minnie's room, a far better night than the many she has endured near the front line in recent months. Refreshed and packed, she is ready to go. I am ready too, everything I own is either on my back or in the bulging Gladstone bag. As soon as Florentina returns from fetching her hat and coat we will leave here for the last time. Nobody knows where James spent the night although he had promised to drop off the costume at the Mariinsky before meeting us at the station this morning to board the train for Moscow and onwards to Archangel. There is no time to lose, the harbour there freezes over at around this time of year.

Leslie has disappeared, sparing us from either a perfunctory or a drawn-out farewell neither of which would have done justice to the mad adventure that has uselessly eaten up the past month of our lives. I resign myself to the fact he is a professional agent not a friend, there is no reason for him to hang around to say goodbye at the end of a job and yet it would have brought a more satisfactory closure to our brief partnership. He has left a large envelope on the table addressed to me in his own hand, my name slanting north-east at an alarming angle which Florentina tells me is a sign of the writer's ambition. A written farewell is perhaps preferable to a verbal one, exact and concise in ways that defy an unscripted dialogue, but I suspect this is just a joke.

Another fat envelope containing empty pages, a cheeky reminder of the blank diplomatic papers I protected with my life on the journey from Vladivostok. But Leslie fools me again, he writes,

> *Travel well, Gordon. The money enclosed should be enough to see you home. It's payment for your work, not a charitable gift. A privilege knowing you, your friend Leslie.*

The pale green, blue and red notes of different shapes and denominations are held together by a rubber band, there must be several thousand roubles altogether. This looks more than enough to pay my passage but I will only remove them from the envelope when I can count them in private.

Mary and I do not look back as we step out of the building into Ofitserskaya Street but Florentina cannot help herself from glancing behind, perhaps to fix this moment forever in her mind. I suspect tears are flowing as she removes a glove and raises a handkerchief to her face as she begins the journey to an unfamiliar foreign nation, the one that Mary and I call home. Florentina is discovering that self-exile is accompanied not only by a sense of anticipation but also by a gnawing regret that will linger, perhaps forever. Minnie, Walter and Frank are ahead of us by over an hour, worried that scheduled departures could be delayed or cancelled throughout the day as chaos in the city rises to new heights. The sooner Walter and Frank can board a train for Moscow the more confident they can be of securing the contract there, being stranded in Petrograd would mean being stranded miles away from their next pay cheque.

I now see this handsome railway station for the first time with my own eyes, it is not long since I was carried through it on a stretcher with my face covered by a white sheet. The clock on the two-storey tower is approaching nine as we enter through the arched doorway below, by this time tomorrow we shall be in Moscow for the rail connection to Archangel. My eye is on the ticket office where James is advancing slowly towards the head of the queue to buy the cheapest seats available, it will not be soft class on this short leg but nobody cares as long as we get out of this cesspit, this once proud city. Florentina is unusually quiet, her decision to leave is weighing more heavily now that Minnie is far down the track on her way back to Omsk where Florentina has friends, a job and a life that was beginning to grow roots. She has just pulled them up.

'No more seats available for today, these tickets are for tomorrow,' James announces impassively.

Florentina's weight leans against my upper arm, I realise she is fainting and manage to support her elbow, breaking a hard fall and letting her sink gracefully down to the floor where she lays on her back. Mary takes charge, placing her shoulder bag under Florentina's feet, loosening the tight-fitting collar around her neck and calmy telling her to stay quiet for a few minutes before trying to move. The flow of travellers in the departure hall splits into two streams as people stop and stare from left and right at the body on the floor, their interest waning as Florentina quickly recovers her senses calling for smelling salts, but nobody is carrying any. Mary recommends essence of valerian to help combat any distress and something to eat, preferably without delay. Florentina insists she is fine, repeatedly reprimanding herself for skipping breakfast and vaguely suggesting we should try the Finland Station instead, where there might be a chance of leaving today instead of tomorrow.

'That would be a journey from hell,' James replies. 'First stop Helsinki, then overland in a huge arc through Finland, Sweden and Norway without any guarantee of getting a berth from Bergen, let alone arriving in Aberdeen without meeting German U boats on the way. We're safer sailing out of the White Sea than straight across the North Sea.'

The room rates in city hotels are beyond our reach, we must conserve our financial resources in case of unexpected expenses on the route home. James is unperturbed by the lack of a bed tonight – he knows the underworld where nobody thinks of sleeping until the last bottle of vodka is empty and the last prostitute on her feet hooks the last client with enough money to get her off them. He hands over our tickets with a promise to meet on the train tomorrow morning, soon not even his hat is visible as he merges with the crowds milling around the exit from the station into Nevsky Avenue. I regret not going with him, it would be more fun than my duty to accompany these two ladies to whatever shelter we can find for the night.

'The Mariinsky Theatre, we'll sleep there,' Florentina proposes, knowing I will not refuse her this time.

CHAPTER 15

THE MARIINSKY

Ofitserskaya Street runs alongside the Mariinsky, there is no telling how Florentina will react to arriving back there after emotionally bidding it a final farewell such a short time ago. Mary and I discuss the risk of her collapsing again. The long walk from the station to the theatre through noisy and excitable crowds marching with their banners aloft will be tiring for her. She has complained of feeling cold. I carry her bag and Mary takes her arm. We shall catch the next tram hoping there will be at least one seat free.

I have passed in front of the theatre before, awed by its monumental proportions I am curious to see the interior. My expectations of entering through the grand central doorway are dashed as Florentina leads us through an unimpressive goods entrance far from the crystal chandeliers and statues adorning the main foyer. The guardian is hunched up like a caged animal in his small workstation where he logs arrivals and departures in the daybook open on the counter. The records for each visitor fill multiple columns: name, age, address, occupation, purpose of visit, proof of identity, time in, time out and delivery chit number if there is one. A roughly written notice on the door announcing the cancellation of tonight's performance explains the absence of entries in the register so far today, nobody has cause to be here. Florentina looks flustered, the monkey face in the cage is unfamiliar, the friendly man she was expecting is off duty. Her sweet-tempered explanations for wanting entry, mention of a close association with the senior wardrobe mistress and the hours spent here on secondment from Omsk creating crowns, pearl tiaras and other accessories worn by members of the ballet company, are met with a grunt. He has no interest in hearing about her contribution to the much-admired headpieces worn by the Snow Maiden, Spring Beauty and Grandfather Frost in Rimsky-Korsakov's opera that has been playing recently on the stage of the Great Hall just a few feet away from the wall behind him. The gatekeeper is an ignorant brute. Without an ounce of compassion for our plight he turns his back on Florentina, puts his feet on the desk, tampers with a row of door keys hanging on the wall to his right, lifts his rump, farts and lights a cigarette. I take Florentina's place at the counter, bang my fist on it and wait for some reaction. When he turns around I lean across to remind him that by a government decree the Mariinsky Theatre has this day been made the property of the State, it is now owned by the People's Enlightenment Commissariat and consequently he has no right to refuse entry to anyone. The days when a petition to the Chancery of the Imperial Theatres was a prerequisite for obtaining a seat in the Mariinsky are over, the time when everyone here was an employee of the Tsar is over too, the theatre now belongs to the people. I threaten to walk out and tell the first group of revolutionaries I can find that a stubborn imperial relic is refusing us entry, a corrupt doorman in the pay of aristocratic opera goers who have lost their old privileges in the new Russia. Finally, he pays attention and waves us through without even recording our names in the daybook.

Florentina guides us along deserted backstage corridors to the green room where performers sit and relax before going on stage. The windowless space is sparsely furnished with worn armchairs, two sofas, small round tables and a large rectangular one where a samovar perches like a wise owl. Her immediate concern is the sleeping arrangements. Pointing to the folded paravent leaning against the wall she announces it will be used to divide the room when the ladies wish to shed their street clothes and doss down on the sofas for the night. She asks me to organise the male sleeping quarters by dragging one of the armchairs into the furthest corner where it can be screened off. The risk of me passing through the ladies' area at night to use the adjacent bathroom seems to be troubling her, she is proposing a warning system that would involve me tapping three times on the dividing screen before emerging from behind it. Florentina might be making such a fuss to impress Mary with her modesty, or she might believe her to be prudish, hardly likely for a nurse familiar with every part of the male anatomy. In any event, it is far too early in the day to be making detailed sleeping and ablutions arrangements, my main concern is food. Mary volunteers to go out looking for provisions, I suggest that old standby the Astoria Hotel kitchen where she can mention Leslie's name and return with whatever is available for our modest budget. Her wink looks like approval of the idea but on reflection it says more about her complicity with my exasperation at Florentina's new-found prissiness. I shall leave her alone to rest but will stay inside the theatre in case that unpredictable doorman decides to lock up and go home without telling us.

The backstage layout is easy enough to fathom even though the house is dark apart from some lamps lit in the distance. Almost every control lever on the lighting switchboard is set to 'off', the counterweights and pulleys are immobilised, long ropes hang limply against the walls and canvases dangle in the fly tower, a vast space where everything fades into oblivion. I touch nothing in this unfamiliar world for fear something unseen will come crashing down on my head. As I step out of the wings onto an eerily silent stage the rake throws me off balance, propelling me faster than expected downstage towards the immense sweep of curtain stretching across the proscenium arch. I waste an audible gasp, there is nobody around to hear it. Nobody to see me running my fingers along the braided edges of the curtains to find the overlap where I can pull them apart, slide through the gap and stand alone on the apron like Fyodor Chaliapin acknowledging an adoring public. Theatrical custom demands I face the lavishly decorated state box, clasp my hands over my heart, extend my arms and then let them fall towards the floor pulling my upper body into a deep bow. I shift slightly to downstage left for a second more deferential, less effusive bow in front of the vacant imperial family box which is only a few feet away. My fantasy curtain-call as Boris Godunov, the Tsar who names his son as heir before expiring to the sounds of monks chanting and the funeral bell pealing, is at an end. Exiting by the stage stair to the stalls, I spare a thought for Nicholas who can never replicate that scene, he wrote himself and his son Alexei out of it when he signed his abdication letter last March.

Clusters of gilded nymphs and cupids observe me walking through the grand hall and up the main staircase where I find the entrance to the state box. Like an outsized picture frame hanging on a hidden hook, it drops from the second tier down to the *belle étage*. Crowned heads, heads of state and heads that found favour with the old regime, their diamonds dancing in the light from the chandelier above, are not welcome here anymore. The stylish chairs have been stacked up with their backs facing the stage. I would give every rouble and kopeck in my pocket to have this view over the auditorium better illuminated, I should have pulled a few levers on the lighting board before coming up here. In the half-light, the stage curtain appears like a ceremonial mantle held in the grip of some ancient god waiting to wrap it around the shoulders of a prima donna assoluta. I have unwittingly and undeservedly bestowed that honour on myself.

I have spent too much time trying to find an access route to the Tsar's family box, my stomach rebels so I hasten back to the greenroom. Mary has returned with plenty of tea leaves but only enough food for one decent meal which we agree to eat in two parts, half now and half later in the evening. Florentina is listless, she rejects solids and is too tired to show us the set design and stage properties workshops, but Mary shares my enthusiasm for setting off to find the Tsar's box. Our request for directions is met with a curt response, the private entrance and staircase are isolated from other parts of the building and the rumours of a secret passage are just rumours. If there are hidden doorways in the Tsar's box and the prima ballerina's dressing room it should be possible to find one of them and follow the passage to the other end, but Florentina is shocked by my audacious suggestion of going to explore. It would be a violation of privacy. Mary winks at me again. We are both curious to investigate the Mariinsky further but Florentina seems to be guarding its secrets as closely as those in her undergarment drawer. The silent stand-off is unresolved until Mary pours two cups of tea, drags a second armchair into the male quarters behind the screen, sits and talks.

'I admire your courage,' I tell her.

'It's work, Gordon. This is what I left home to do, knowing there would be hardships. It helps being part of a group of like-minded people, the Scottish nurses are a resilient bunch.'

'What you do is more of a calling than just work. This is altruism.'

'You flatter me. I nurse broken bodies and write to bereaved families.'

'How do you find the words?'

'They find me. I always write that everything possible was done, every remedy was tried but to no avail. Sometimes I add that he had a smile and a cheery word up to the very last, sometimes I say how fearfully upset

I am. Once I wrote that I'm certain he went straight to heaven.'

'Only once?'

'Yes, he was very special. His death was strangely beautiful.'

I expect Mary to start weeping but she is composed, fleetingly enigmatic, part way on a journey to another world. A moment that commands silence until I can be sure she has returned to this planet.

'Do you receive any replies?' I ask, hoping the question will not upset her.

'I don't even know if my letters arrive. I simply try to make things better, isn't that the whole point of being on this Earth?'

'Not everybody thinks like that. Some only look after themselves, some make mischief, others have to follow orders without question even if it makes things worse.'

'And you?'

'I catch thermals.'

'The atmosphere is unstable these days, were you blown off course, is that why you're here?'

'Blown off course is an understatement. Hoodwinked would be more accurate.'

'Well, we must look forward not backwards. Where next?'

'Scotland to see my grandparents and then Yorkshire to stay with my parents. I have been away from home too long. I expect to see many changes.'

'Does that frighten you?'

'Frighten me? No. Like you, I walked away knowing nothing would ever be the same again.'

'Scotland will be the same. I'm the one that's changed, that's what frightens me.'

'How?'

'Less carefree.'

'Would you do it all again?'

Mary pauses. She leans forward, her clasped hands pressed tight between her knees, looks at me quizzically and then giggles.

'Don't be so stupid, of course I would,' she replies.

I am unaccustomed to any woman except my mother calling me stupid. When Mary realises the word has had an unintended effect on me, she switches subject.

'You talk about your grandparents and your parents, how about your wife and children, aren't you looking forward to seeing them when you get back?'

'I am not married.'

'You must be the first unmarried man I've met who wears a wedding ring.'

'More evidence of my stupidity, I'm afraid.'

'It's a difficult disease to cure but it can be done,' she jokes.

'The prognosis is poor in my case. This is the Tsar's ring.'

'Goodness me, I didn't realise I'm in such elevated company. Are you wearing stolen property?'

'It's just a curtain ring.'

'Tell me more.'

'He wears a wedding ring, so I had to wear one too.'

'Frankly, I don't see that much resemblance between you and the Tsar but perhaps you could have got away with it. James persuaded me to be on hand to mop up your blood but if the damned stupid plan had gone ahead I'd be doing more than that. I'd be writing to your family by now.'

'With or without a mention of going straight to heaven?'

'I would have written pages about you deserving a long spell in purgatory to atone for your stupidity, no doubt about that. So, when will you be removing that curtain ring?'

'I shall be getting a replacement soon. I have a fiancée. We plan to marry early next year.'

A rustling from the other side of the screen turns into the heavy sound of Florentina tossing and turning on the sofa.

'I can't sleep when you talk so loud. *Sottovoce per favore,'* Florentina pleads feebly.

'Why the Italian?' Mary whispers to me.

'She is half Italian, but I suspect it's done for theatrical effect,' I whisper back.

We instinctively draw the two chairs closer together until the arms are almost touching. Mary sits forward and turns her head as if to lip read, I do likewise. Our eyes work in harmony with our ears, not a word gets lost as we natter quietly into the night.

Mary is an only child – her widowed mother works as an assistant in a bootmaker's shop to the west of the Scott Monument on Princes Street. Although I visited Edinburgh many years ago with Granny Smith I have no recollection of the shops, all the excitement for a boy is on the opposite side of the road. Granny told me stories of kings, queens, plots and murders as we walked up the hill from Holyrood Palace on our way to the castle, but we never got that far. She decided to stop at St

Giles Cathedral to say a prayer for a sick relative, an unwanted answer or one of her peculiar premonitions meant we set off in haste directly to the infirmary in Lauriston Place instead of going to the castle. We arrived at the infirmary too late, left Edinburgh earlier than planned, Granny went into mourning and I turned glum because I had been looking forward to seeing the cannons and battlements. She spoke little on our journey home except for encouraging me to study medicine in Edinburgh, or Glasgow like my father. I wondered at the time why she would even mention such a future, surely there could be no other.

'So, your father is a doctor.'

'Yes, he is now a general practitioner. Soon after graduating he did some research work with an English surgeon and they produced a paper on some particularly revolting case of worms. It was published in one of the leading medical journals.'

'That case sounds familiar, it was studied by trainee nurses when I was at the Royal Infirmary. A middle-aged doctor was invited to lecture about it, he was a co-author if I recall correctly.'

'Do you remember his name?'

'It must be ten years ago now. I might know the name if someone mentioned it.'

'Does the name Doctor Reynolds mean anything to you?'

'No. I remember more about the case than the doctor who presented it. The woman was in her thirties, about four months pregnant with chest and abdominal pains, vomiting up worms. She discharged them through the rectum and nostrils too with profuse losses of blood. Some crawled into the Eustachian tubes, perforated the ear membranes and were pulled out by a queasy husband.'

'Not the kind of lecture one forgets.'

'Seventy-four.'

'I thought you said he was middle-aged, not an old man.'

'Worms, seventy-four worms. I remember that fact clearly. The doctor must have been in his mid-fifties, which probably seemed ancient to us young students.'

'Was it Dr Dickson by any chance?'

'Yes, that's it. I remember now, he started the lecture by talking about the importance of distinguishing between verifiable and unverifiable information. "When a fact is ascertainable, make sure you ascertain it, don't just guess," he said. "I'm an *icks* not an *ix*, that much is ascertainable." Nobody understood him until he pointed out that his name had been mis-spelt on the lecture programme.'

'That sounds just like my father, he hates it when he sees his name spelt incorrectly.'

'Doctor Dickson is your father?'

'Yes. John Dickson. A bit of a dry stick but mellowing with age.'

'My father always said Scotland is a village, he keeps being proved right. I miss him, he was an engineer on the railways, killed stone dead when an engine skipped the points. My poor mother had difficulty making ends meet until she inherited some money from a great aunt, a spinster with an untouched nest egg.'

There is not much left of the night. Mary returns to her sofa on tiptoe to catch some sleep. Our long journey home begins early tomorrow morning. I cannot get

comfortable enough in this armchair to enjoy a restor-
ative nap, I have been sitting here too long ignoring the
pain in my leg which always worsens without regular
exercise. Running around the room is not an option, the
only solution is to strip down to my loose-fitting flannel
drawers and perform a few squats without wakening
the ladies. But Mary has not fallen asleep, she returns
to find out why I am so restless. I tell her the story of
my injury during the Boxer riots, we discuss the effi-
cacy of Chinese traditional medicines and in particular
those Ling used to heal my leg and calm the pain. In the
semi-darkness it is impossible to see clearly enough for
an examination of the scar tissue, so I guide her hand
along the length and breadth of the smooth raised welt
on my thigh.

'I could have done a better job of repairing that
gash,' Mary murmurs into my ear.

'The conditions were basic, no doctor on hand, no
needle, no stitches. I was lucky not to get a bad infec-
tion. The young person who helped me was barely a
teenager, she did her best. That teenager is now a
woman, that woman will soon be my bride.'

'We have plenty of time to talk tomorrow, I must
go back to my sofa now.'

This morning Mary and I pack quickly, Florentina is
distracted. I worry she will delay our departure for the
station.

'Do actors get time calls?' I ask her.

'Yes, the "overture and beginners" call is the first
one. It concerns the musicians and actors who must be
on stage when the curtain goes up,' Florentina replies.

'Well, this is a call to get away from here. Curtain up in ten minutes.' I know we have closer to fifteen but adding a margin does no harm.

Florentina fails to respond, motionless apart from twisting the end of her scarf around her fingers she finally finds the courage to speak.

'I will not be coming with you.'

'Why the sudden change of heart?'

'It's not sudden, Gordon. I have slept on it and decided the idea is madness.'

I try to reassure Florentina that she will be well looked after when we arrive in Britain, my grandparents have a spare room she can use until she finds a permanent lodging. They will be pleased to have young blood in the house.

'You are very caring, but I fear the same fate as the Snow Maiden.'

'What happened to her?' Mary asks.

'The Snow Maiden lived with an old couple, they were kind to her and she helped them. But she was sad at home, unable to find love she left them in search of it. When her heart warmed, she melted. Some women are not meant for love, they should not seek it. I am one of them. A chill descends on every hope of romance I have ever had. I felt that chill again last night.'

'One should never lose hope,' Mary says, trying to give Florentina a boost.

'My hopes get pushed further into the future, further into the shade. So many young men sent to war, so few who have returned.' Florentina sniffles.

'You are not at fault, don't be upset. We find peace by coming to terms with reality, by following our instincts, you must follow yours.' Mary takes her hand, pulling her close.

'I have realised that my life is here where every-thing is make-believe, a place where I can pretend to be in love and make it almost real. I will always love the characters, the voices and the music, I will never melt for as long as the theatre is my home.'

'Florentina, I hate to leave you like this, but we must go now.'

'I understand, Gordon. I will show you out.'

Florentina directs her wan smile at the floor, bids us farewell and tugs at the handle on the door where we entered the theatre yesterday. It appears to have jammed but on closer inspection the lock has been turned and the key removed. The guardian must have locked up, to my dismay all the keys have been taken down from their hooks and hidden away somewhere. The small-minded man has taken his revenge by trap-ping us inside the building, there is no telling when he will return. I supress the expletives I would have rel-ished using had I been alone with Leslie and do my best to remain calm. Perhaps Florentina knows of another exit route. She dismisses the possibility of the main en-trance where there are multiple locks, the stage door must be firmly shut too, nobody has been in or out of it for more than twenty-four hours. Access to the scene dock is padlocked by the stage manager himself, he would never let that key off his chain, never let that chain off his belt and only remove his belt at home. I ask if there are any traps in the stage that might lead us to underground passageways with openings to the out-side world but Florentina doubts it. In any event we do not have time to waste on dead ends, we need a quick, reliable solution.

'Follow me,' Florentina commands in a strong confident voice.

She leads us back along the corridor towards the green room, threads her way through the wings and into the prima ballerina's dressing room. Pots of make-up, hairbrushes, clips and false braids cover the dressing table, a white tutu hangs from a hook and several pairs of ballet shoes are lined neatly on the floor. A hardwood barre, running along the length of the room at waist height, is attached by simple brackets to the mirrored wall behind. The thin cut dividing the barre into two unequal parts is barely visible until Florentina pulls gently on the shorter section. The full-length mirror behind it swings open, without making a noise, to reveal a narrow passageway. She leads us in single file along it into the imperial family box, up a few red-carpeted steps, through a succession of richly decorated antechambers and to the private door leading onto the street. Florentina is not surprised to find it locked. Two heavily patterned silk curtains swing down across the door when Florentina disengages the chunky tie backs that have been holding them aside. The gold and blue braided reef ropes with four huge tassels, two on each loop, lay in her outstretched arms like a precious newborn being presented for baptism.

'With luck, we should find a door key sewn into the middle of one of these tassels.'

'Why would anyone sew a key into a tassel?' I ask.

'Don't waste precious time, just help us to find it,' Mary replies whilst performing a palpation deep in the fringes of the first one. 'Nothing abnormal,' she declares as if examining for a suspected appendicitis.

'Keep looking,' Florentina urges. 'I know that a key has been secreted close to this door in case of an emergency such as a fire or a riot that could threaten the lives of the imperial family. The Empress did not trust any of the guards to stay on duty and awake throughout the five hours of her husband's favourite Wagnerian opera, *Tristan and Isolde*. Never sure which guards would remain loyal, never sure who would be susceptible to bribery, she demanded a door key for her personal use. It was impractical to carry it to and from the theatre in her gem encrusted reticule hence a lady-in-waiting to the Tsarina instructed that a key be sewn into a tassel. Bertha, here at the time on secondment as a senior seamstress, was assigned the task only five minutes before leaving the theatre on her way back home to Omsk. She realised the timing was to lessen the risk of her gossiping with colleagues about the key and as far as I know she never talked about it to anyone except me. She could not resist sharing her suspicion that it opens this door. These tassels fit her description. The key must still be here.'

'Providing nobody removed it after the abdication,' I add.

'I doubt it has gone, so few people know about it,' Florentina replies in a rare moment of optimism.

'I have it,' Mary shouts holding up her second attempt, 'we need scissors.'

'It's not an umbilical cord, just bring the whole thing to the door, we don't need to cut the key off,' I answer.

Mary and I step out into the street. I turn around to bid farewell, intending to say a word of thanks and wish Florentina luck, but the door has closed. Finickity by nature, she will soon have replaced everything exactly as we found it, the curtains will be taken prisoner again by the tie backs and the tassels hanging just-so with the hidden key seemingly undisturbed. The imperial family box will fall quiet as if it had never been violated, nothing suspicious will be reflected in the dressing room mirrors, only the green room will be occupied. Florentina will spend the morning alone there with her thoughts, her eyes moist with regret at refusing the challenge of a new life in a foreign country, reddening at the prospect of her world shrinking to the size of a theatre building.

My principal concern is to find James amongst the crowds in the station. Mary and I hurry along the platform where the train for Moscow is blowing steam. He should be waiting here but neither of us can spot him, my inclination is to board and devil take the hindmost. We cannot afford to miss the train, if James has had a heavy night and stayed in bed too long this morning that is not our problem.

'Gord-en,' he shouts from behind me. As I turn round, he is standing there on the carriage steps waving his arms as if yelling my name would not be enough to gain my attention. 'Time is getting short. I boarded thinking you were already on the train. Where is Florentina?'

'She is not coming with us. The poor soul is in turmoil, not knowing which way to go.'

'Where is she now?'

'We left her at the Mariinsky.'

'The Mariinsky? I must get her out of there.'

'You'll miss the train if you do that. Archangel will be icing up any day now. We cannot hang around here.'

'Finding her is more important than anything that might be happening at Archangel.'

'Her mind is made up. She is not leaving Russia.'

'I thought you said she doesn't know which way to go.'

'True, until this morning, but now her choice has been made. She wants to spend her life working in the theatre.'

'She is in danger.'

James gathers his belongings and steps onto the platform, his voice breathless in anticipation of rushing off to the Mariinsky. It seems that the doorman who played with us like mice is not the lazy state employee we assumed him to be. James has been drinking in the seedy bars gathering intelligence since we parted company, loose talk of a bloated body found in the canal three days ago is no longer just gossip. It has been identified as the friendly doorman Florentina had expected to meet at the Mariinsky. A bullet in his head signals nothing uncommon, there have been many such deaths during the chaos of the last months, but his replacement at the Mariinsky has James and his camaraderie of night owls hooting with indignation. The man who now guards the theatre door is a German sympathiser, a thief, drunkard and a rapist known in the underworld as both perverted and violent. Leaving the fragile Florentina alone with him in a dark theatre is inconceivable.

'That changes everything, we will go with you to rescue her,' I tell James.

'No. Leave it to me and my friends, we are perfectly capable of dealing with him. You go ahead with Mary. Perhaps we'll meet again, perhaps not. Safe travels.'

CHAPTER 16

BINNIEHILL HOUSE

Archangel harbour is congested with vessels, goods are being hauled on and off the quayside by navvies hoarse with shouting, unseasoned timber is arriving from the rail terminal, bagged grain is stacked high, and the warehouses cannot swallow anything more. The cold air nips at our cheeks as Mary and I queue to embark a hired military transport ship sailing in convoy for Aberdeen. Mary's paperwork is in order but mine is being questioned, forgeries are rife, only the very best can fool the authorities.

'Of course, he's a doctor,' Mary tells the inspector. 'Doctor Dickson is a celebrated medical researcher in my country. He is held in high regard.'

I face an interrogation about my research. After trotting out everything I know about worms crawling through bodily orifices I show the official the faded name of 'John Dickson' debossed in the leather of my father's Gladstone bag. He is confused by the letters FRCSE. Mary explains them with an uncharacteristic air of superiority calculated to bring the cross-examination to a halt with irrefutable evidence that I am a Fellow of the Royal College of Surgeons, Edinburgh. She is unsuccessful. The question of my middle name arises, I am required to justify the reason for it appearing on my travel documents but not on the bag. Mary begins a convoluted story about clan names staying constant throughout generations and therefore 'Gordon' is optional on the bag, but my given name 'John' is not. This is incomprehensible to the official and it begins to confuse me too, I try a more prosaic approach.

'Do you know how much it costs to have a name debossed in leather? The charge per letter is exorbitant. I am not rich enough or stupid enough to waste money on having the name Gordon on my bag when everyone knows me as John.'

We are now the only two passengers still waiting to embark. My hope of joining the ship is slipping away and despite my insistence Mary refuses to board without me. She makes a show of opening her bag to reach for a small vial of patchouli oil, and when she dabs a drop behind each ear the sensual fragrance makes me smile but it fails to charm the crocodile of a man who still has me writhing in his grip. Unlikely as it seems, if I were to be unmasked as a player in a plot to rescue the Tsar, I could be here for a very long time. Mary and I are running out of strategies as we become aware of James standing behind us, he takes quick stock of the situation, taps my shoulder and greets me warmly.

'Doctor John Dickson, how wonderful to meet again. Going home?'

'Aye, I hope so,' I reply.

The guard waves Mary and me through with a perfunctory flip of the wrist accompanied by a scowl.

'There are no more berths on this sailing but with luck I'll find something soon. Florentina is safely out of the Mariinsky and on her way to ...' James is yelling at the top of his voice, but Mary and I are already on the gangplank too far away to catch the end of his sentence.

This ship used to carry passengers between Southampton and New York, the privileged in magnificent first-class cabins, two hundred in cabin class and the masses down below in steerage. Following a re-fit several years ago there is no longer any first-class accommodation, but Mary has the good fortune to be sharing a comfortable cabin on the second-highest deck with another nurse. My lot is steerage. Men with little means are berthed forward on the two lowest decks in compartments designed for groups of twenty, ten berths down each side of the hull with an open space in the middle furnished with a long table used for meals, card games and banter. I have the use of a small locker, blankets are provided and although I would prefer to be at the end of a row my allocated bunk is in the middle, not far from the head. I have no expectation of seeing Mary throughout the voyage, my only company will be the assorted types jostling around in this confined space, each one measuring up the others. This is far from luxury but also far from the misery of conditions reported by transatlantic emigrants of twenty years ago, there are stewards on call, showering is possible for a fee, soap and towels are provided, and the smell of bleach is strong enough to keep rats and mice away. I will be out on the open deck as often as possible sniffing the sea spray, there is limited access up there for steerage passengers, but I count on many of them staying below playing poker.

Ice is beginning to form around the port but it will not hamper the scheduled departure, we shall be out in the Arctic Ocean and rounding the North Cape before it sets thick enough to close off this inland sea until next spring. The voyage is likely to be tedious, there are only five hours of daylight this far north at this time of the year, and dangerous too. German U boats are patrolling out there in the depths looking for convoys like this one, I have little faith that our six-inch guns guarantee a safe passage, vast amounts of tonnage have been sunk in this war with a great loss of lives. Dwelling on the risks is pointless. All aboard are at the mercy of the captain, the crew and the elements, there is nothing to be achieved by worrying, the only precaution possible is paying attention to emergency procedures. I can take refuge in my thoughts, detach myself from reality and confine myself to the world as it will be when Ling and I are settled and start a family. I imagine her somewhere on an ocean too, preparing for arrival in a foreign land, unsure of local customs, anxious about meeting my parents and wary of shocking them with her foreign manners. At least her name and the critical role she played in saving my life from those crazy Boxers are familiar to my relatives, Ling is not a total stranger to them. My mother would not have accepted anyone without a good Christian upbringing marrying into the family and by extension my father would write me out of his will should I dare to choose someone of a different faith. Ling does not face any opposition on that score, but I have some apprehension about her wedding dress. I can hear the intake of breath as she walks down the aisle dressed in red, the traditional colour for brides in her country, the whispers of scarlet woman, the shock throughout the entire village community. I must protect her from any such humiliation.

Men are starting to move aft to the galley. I am not feeling hungry but fear if I miss this opportunity there will be no more food on offer until the morning by which time my stomach will be empty. The queue waiting to be served moves slowly. The nearer I get to the front the stronger the smell of fish becomes, those circling back to eat at the long table are each carrying a mess tin overflowing with a greyish slurry and a portion of black bread. I overhear them rejoicing that fresh fish stew is being served, from tomorrow there will only be pickled herring, dried reindeer, salt pork or bully. I prefer to eat in silence but the young man to my right insists on talking, whether or not his mouth is empty. Ewen is loud, he casts his net wide in the hope of attracting the attention of at least one person at the table who might be willing to share stories throughout the night, someone willing to pull out a bottle of alcohol concealed somewhere in the depths of a hidden haversack.

He talks about his unhappy childhood south of Falkirk, truancy and signing up for a life at sea to escape from becoming a fourth-generation miner. When the coal boom started, men could easily find work in the collieries, Ewen's great-grandfather was one of them. The job was hard, accidents were commonplace, the pay was barely enough to raise a family, the hastily built miners' cottages where Ewen, his father and grandfather were all born on the kitchen floor, were never anything better than damp and cramped hovels. When the mines opened the whole community thought that demand for high-quality domestic coal would last. Nobody doubted that the railway wagons filled beyond the brim with pyramids of black gold would forever trundle off from the mine-head towards Ireland and other distant markets. The monotony, the pride in doing a job that put food on the table and the sense of community were the fabric of daily life. Ewen preaches about those old days as if he were handing down the fifth gospel from his great-grandfather, history lessons that must have been repeated countless times by the elders to give the youngsters a sense of their roots. Ewen's father knew all about mines before he first went down one at the age of fourteen, he had grown up recognising his own father's face whether it was black with grime or pink with scrubbing. The men rose early day after day to work underground, slow to realise that above them the value of their output was beginning to collapse due to a fall in demand. Ewen's cheeks take on the colour of his red hair, spittle flies as he curses the coalmasters for cutting miners' wages by sixpence per day in response to the falling coal prices. The men went out on strike in protest.

'Those bastard coalmasters counted on starvation driving the men back to work. They tried to evict families, drag them from their homes, folk were helpless, living in squalor and hungry every day. The strike was in its sixth week when the miners heard ejectment notices were being served, full of fury they marched behind the brass band from Limerigg to Slamannan to settle scores. When they got to Binniehill, the coalmaster's house, they trashed it inside and out, the parlour, the windows, the greenhouse and the flowerpots were smashed. Nobody could stop them. A fine job of work they did that day. Nothing was stolen. Imagine that, honest to a man.'

My mind is spinning. My grandfather is coalmaster, he and Granny Smith live at Binniehill House. How is this possible, has something happened in my absence, is this calamity some terrible family secret? How could my God-fearing grandfather behave like this, crushing his fellow man into submission?

'Terrible business. No wonder you ran away to sea,' I say in the hope of hearing more without asking him directly.

'Running away was easy. Got to go for a piss,' he announces brightly to all as he leaves the table holding his crotch like a four-year-old boy who waited too long.

When he returns his place next to me has been taken, I will have to wait for another opportunity to continue the conversation. The man now sitting in Ewen's seat is driving himself mad trying to work out why it is the end of November in Archangel but mid-December in Scotland. I explain the difference between the Julian and Gregorian calendars but to no avail, he grumbles at having been deprived of the thirteen days lost to him forever. My patience with his nonsense reaches its limits, the fast forward in time tormenting him changes nothing in my plans. Binniehill is still within reach before Christmas, heaven only knows what I will find when I get there.

I wear every piece of clothing I possess, washing once a day to preserve a minimum standard of hygiene. I wish my fellow travellers would do likewise, the ventilation is poor, the sea is getting rough, nobody is allowed up on deck, and this place is beginning to stink of rancid humanity. The hull groans along a centre line from bow to stern as the vessel repeatedly lurches upward and forward on the waves, swirls and crashes down. The propeller must be continually out of the water, the waves must be towering over the ship but all I see of the storm is a stream running through the hatchway and random items floating around on the floor. Most of the men are in their bunks, a few hardy fools are at the table but when one of them projects the meal he has just finished straight back into the empty mess tin, the others lose their appetites. I've started to feel like a cat with hairballs, the urge to throw up gets stronger, my stomach empties and empties again until cramps set in. The headache is relentless, there is no sign of the sea calming, we are all at the mercy of whatever god we believe in and for my part a U boat would bring a welcome end to it all. The steward distributes life belts before hurriedly beating a retreat, the chances of making it to Aberdeen are narrowing by the hour. Nobody speaks, the only human sounds are retching and moaning, but the fear is almost tangible. There is no sign of when or how this will end, I cannot recall a storm comparable to this one during my travels to China and Japan. I will be just one of thousands in the alphabetical list of those lost at sea in December 1917, a sobering thought for the long night ahead. In truth, I cannot be sure whether the night or the day lies ahead, there will be no relief until sleep comes, the storm abates or the ship breaks up and everyone aboard is consigned to Davy Jones' locker.

A man is reported overboard. A lifeboat has been lost, the bolts fixing the winch foundation were ruptured by the force of water, and there is much cleaning up to be done now that the worst of the storm has passed. We will soon be south of Shetland. Home begins to feel close and yet there are still dangers. Mines are a threat. It is only a few weeks ago that two British destroyers and nine merchant ships carrying coal were sunk off Lerwick by German cruisers. Losses of all kinds are the main topic of conversation amongst the men – a family member killed in the war, a severed limb or a love affair recounted in the past tense. I wait to hear Ewen's story of loss before realising he is no longer in his bunk or at the table, the young man who refused to go down a mine is the one who was washed over the handrail after disobeying orders to stay below. His mother will be beside herself. His father and grandfather will lament his passing, united in an unsteady conviction that the boy was too headstrong and should have been given the strap more often for his own good, it could have saved his life. He would be down the mine with them today instead of down on the seabed alone.

We are allowed up on deck at last, the sea is calm, the ship is making good progress. Men are guessing when the British coastline will come into view, betting a tanner to register the date and time when they fancy that land will be sighted. I have been appointed bookie. I note down the punters' names, the day, hour and minute of their choosing and I hold the winner-takes-all kitty which has reached almost one pound. Several men have made multiple bets. I have not placed one myself, which by general agreement qualifies me as a suitable arbiter in the event of any dispute. Someone at the back of the crowd can be overheard saying a medical doctor can be trusted to act fairly and therefore nobody can object to my final ruling on the result. A pair of binoculars changes hands at ten-minute intervals to ensure that every player has a fair shot at scanning the skyline for something other than an optical illusion. A couple of optimists have put money on a time before dusk, most bets are bunched during daylight tomorrow and one weary soul has given up hope of seeing land until Sunday.

The winner is 8.45 a.m. on Friday. Dawn is rising on my homeland, the ship will be docking before lunchtime, I will board a Caledonian line train from Aberdeen via Perth to Slamannan and be knocking on the front door of Binniehill House by early afternoon. The decks are crammed with excited passengers, cheers go up and people start singing accompanied by an amateur musician playing his trombone to the seagulls. A church elder gathers folk together for prayers of thanksgiving and remembrance, I join the group to honour Ewen's memory but pay little attention to the words being spoken. My mind is back in Russia where the peasants must still be chiding their god for being a long way up and their Tsar for being a long way off. Their sense of abandonment is deep, I cannot help thinking that my failure to help rescue the Tsar means he will never again be close to the simple people who love him.

The steerage-class passengers are the last to disembark. I harbour hopes of finding Mary amongst the hundreds of people milling around but eventually concede she must already be on her way to Edinburgh. Perhaps it is better to have avoided an emotional farewell, my feelings for her until now have been kept in check by the commitment I made to Ling. Mary can be nothing more than a friend to me.

The train passed through Glenellrig without stopping and arrived in Slamannan a few minutes after. There is nothing much of note here apart from a tiny station with a weathered wooden canopy, an oversized lantern and a huge advertisement covering most of the gable end, like everything else the words on the wall 'VIM Cleanser and Polisher' are dusted with soot. The flimsy gates are still juddering over the railway-crossing now the train has disappeared at a vanishing point on the track leading to Airdrie. I breathe in the heavy air and look around. A man is sitting in the small red brick signal box on the opposite side of the empty platform looking back at me. He raises a hand to the peak of his cap and smiles. I have never felt more at home.

I walk less than a mile from the station to where High Street becomes Bank Street. The lodge gates are open but Binniehill House itself remains hidden down a long driveway running past the neighbours at Gowanlee and Strattenhouse. At the turning circle where the drive curls round on itself, I catch a glimpse of the slate roof and wide eaves towering above the quiet and colourless garden. I remember a wedding reception being held here for the minister of the Free Church in Slamannan and his bride who is an aunt of mine. A marquee had been erected on the lawn, the borders were in full bloom, there was music and dancing, it was the talk of the village. But everything is still and monochrome today apart from a figure in the distance wearing a purple shawl. It cannot be Granny Smith, in her late seventies and suffering from arthritis she is unlikely to be pottering around at the far end of the garden on a cold December day. As I approach, the woman is reaching into a holly bush cutting branches, she is too busy to notice me until the crunch of my boots on the gravel startles her.

'Can I help you?' she shouts.

'Yes, I hope so. I'm looking for Binniehill House,' I shout back.

'Well, you don't have far to go. This is it.'

'Does the coalmaster live here?'

'He does indeed but he's away on business in Falkirk today. Can you return tomorrow?'

'I've come a long way to visit him and his wife.'

'She's at home but I doubt she will receive a stranger.'

'Would Granny Smith refuse to see her grandson?'

'Gordon?' The slight woman in the shawl shrieks in disbelief. 'What is the world coming to when I don't recognise my own brother? You've lost so much weight and it looks as though you haven't shaved for days. Why didn't you write? We've had no news from you for almost a year. Is everything alright?'

'Don't worry about me, I'm fine. How are you?'

'I'll be better when I get these branches in some glycerine and hot water. I don't want the leaves curling and the berries falling off before Christmas day.'

'I see the windows have been repaired.'

'What are you talking about?'

'The miners' strike, the rioting, all that damage done to the house and garden. I heard about it last week.'

'Whoever told you is a little behind the times. That happened when Mr McKillop was the coalmaster living here. Back in those days, Grandpa was still running his grocery business at Crossburn House. Come inside, I have hot vegetable and pearl barley soup on the stove. You look as though you need some.'

I shadow Gertie along the path, under the whalebone arch and around the side of the house to the kitchen entrance. She has always been a stickler for order and cleanliness – I remove my dirty boots at the door without being asked and drop my single piece of luggage next to them. I cannot wait to satisfy my hunger, but Gertie insists I wash and change into clean clothes, a luxury I do not possess, before sitting at the kitchen table.

'I'll bring a fresh shirt and underwear from Grandpa's wardrobe. They'll be too big for you but not by much. Leave your jacket and trousers outside the bathroom, I can brush them and buff up your boots whilst you go for a wash.'

The pedestal sink and clawfoot tub are exactly as I remember them. This is an indulgence I have not enjoyed since travelling in soft class, my new self is ready for food and then I want to see Granny.

'Tell me about your travels.'

'I'll talk about them when Grandpa returns this evening then I don't have to say everything twice. I didn't expect to find you here, I thought you would be with mother and father in Yorkshire.'

'I'm staying at Binniehill to look after Granny. Grandpa is well and fiercely independent, but Granny has her good days and bad days.'

'How bad?'

'Often confused, some memory loss but cheerful enough. At least there have been no mood changes, on a good day she is still her adorable feisty self.'

'Is she bedridden?'

'Goodness, no. She stays in the parlour during the day. I keep the fire stoked. She wraps herself in a rug, sits in an armchair whistling to the flames through her dentures, recites nonsense rhymes to the dog and eats two hearty meals a day with Grandpa and me in the dining room. I take her a pot of tea around three o'clock. When the warmer weather comes, I expect she will want to sit and drink her tea in the garden. That will make it more difficult, I shall have to keep an eye on her and make sure she doesn't wander off to the village by herself.'

'I'll take tea with her this afternoon.'

'Tomorrow, wait for tomorrow. She's not having the best of days.'

'I've learned not to wait for anything. There is nothing to be gained by it. The world doesn't know you're waiting, does it? It just keeps turning. Carpe diem.'

'Tell that to the young women waiting for their sweethearts to return from this lousy war. Spinsters spend a whole lifetime waiting with nothing to show at the end of it.'

'Precisely my point. If Granny is not feeling well, I will only spend five minutes with her.'

'Where do you inherit this stubbornness from? Do as you please, I'll prepare tea and buns for two, but before you go in let me tell her she has a visitor.'

'I don't want to give her a heart attack, could the shock be too much for her?'

'Strong as an ox, no need to worry about that.'

Gertie leaves the parlour shaking her head with confirmation that Granny is living deep in her own world reciting 'Strim, strim, strama diddle,' the nonsense rhyme she used to love telling us as children. As I enter, Jack Russell, her lame Labrador named after some ancestor, is stretched out on the rug. He barely raises his head, looks at me with disdain and lets it drop to the floor again. His minor stirring is the cue for Granny to speak from the depths of her wingback armchair even before I have closed the parlour door behind me.

'How nice to have a visitor, my second this week. Come in dear, pull up a chair.'

The voice is strong and clear. A high lace collar and the long sleeves of a green jacket cover any signs of ageing that her neck and wrists might otherwise reveal. She is dressed as smartly as ever. A ruby ring set with diamonds, a family heirloom, catches the light as four of her fingers rub the painful knuckles on her other hand. The ebony handle of a walking stick poking out from behind the embroidered cushion she has at her side is a sign of some physical decline, but Granny has aged less than I expected. The tea tray has been placed safely on a small round table within her reach. I sit facing this proud, elderly woman for whom I have unbounded affection, lean forward to align my regard with hers and hope for her pale blue eyes to light up when she recognises me. They do but only by a little.

'Kenneth, how kind of you to visit. You have not been to see me for such a long time.'

I am slow to respond.

'I have been looking forward so much to seeing you. My work has kept me away from Scotland but now we can spend time together and share stories.'

'When Gertie told me my grandson was here, I could hardly believe it. I want to hear all your news.'

'I'm pleased to see you looking so well. Gertie told me that Eleanor and John will be here for Hogmanay.'

'Eleanor?'

'Yes, your eldest daughter. The one with four children, Gordon, Connie, Gertie and Kenneth, who died.'

'Kenneth died?'

'Yes, when he was only one year old. I'm Gordon.'

'Of course, the one who left home to travel abroad. I was so sad when you went away. I remember saying "Don't go, Gordon" but young men never listen.'

'Well, I'm not such a young man anymore.'

'You are back safe. My prayers have been answered, "Lord watch between me and thee, when we are absent from one another." Back safe and you came to see me. How kind. I had another visitor a few days ago.'

'I expect you have many. How long have you lived in this house, almost twenty-five years? Everybody in the village must know you.'

'My visitor wasn't from the village. She came from afar, one of those countries where people eat a lot of rice. I know the name, but it escapes me.'

'Japan?'

'No, the other one.'

'China?'

'Yes, China. She told me her name, it sounded foreign, but I can't in the life of me recall it. The tea we are drinking is a gift from her, imagine that! In any event, she asked for you and wanted to wait.'

'Wait here for me?'

'Yes, I found it very strange. I asked her to go away, but she refused.'

'Where is she now?'

'I told her to go back to where she came from. I said a telegram had arrived a fortnight ago informing the family of Gordon's death from double pneumonia in Petrograd. I had to tell a little white lie to get rid of her. She was distraught which strengthened my resolve, we don't like to show our emotions in this family. Anyway, I decided to sooth her distress by saying the nurse who looked after him in Petrograd had written a very sweet letter saying she was sure Gordon went straight to heaven.'

'Why wouldn't you let her wait for me?'

'Kenneth dear, have you forgotten? Your cousin Christina, her husband and their wee laddie, God bless them all, were beheaded by the Chinese.'

ACKNOWLEDGEMENTS

Great-uncle Gordon died thirty years before I was born. I cannot recall his name ever being mentioned by his sister (my grandmother) or by my father and his siblings. I only took an interest in his life because my parents gave me Dickson as a middle name. It was a curious choice, but they had already used up other names that run in the family. My brothers got them before I arrived.

When Gordon's mother died in 1960, I inherited her illuminated diary. I was fascinated by her handwritten entries for 1 and 8 November because they referred to a man with my name.

> *1 *John Gordon Dickson 1879*
>
> *8 *Died in Petrograd Novr. 8th 1917 aged 38 years & interred in Lutheran cemetery there*

(The asterisks against the dates were clearly added when Eleanor recorded her son's death).

It is thanks to David Whitford, who organised research and visits in St Petersburg, that I have details not only of the burial plot in Petrograd but also other facts relating to Gordon's time in Russia. On a wet October day in 2018 I took my wife, Christine, to the muddy cemetery to look for Gordon's grave. Any wooden cross that might have been placed there in late 1917 was long gone but the visit was memorable, especially for my wife. It was her birthday.

I am grateful to Helen Rappaport who kindly responded to a message I sent her in October 2017 after reading her book *Caught in the Revolution*. Helen was instrumental in spurring further research into Gordon's life.

A collaboration between Richard Davies (the Leeds Russian Archive at the University of Leeds) and Michael Welch, produced detailed information about circumstances and locations that would otherwise have escaped me. I appreciate their efforts and the time so generously given to satisfying my curiosity on many points, including the hospitals and nursing homes in Petrograd. I am deeply indebted to Richard for correcting errors in the draft manuscript, notably those pertaining to Russian culture and history.

Michael unearthed correspondence between Dr John Dickson, Gordon's father, and the Foreign Office following Gordon's death. I credit him with the joy I had seeing my great-grandfather's elegant handwriting for the first time.

Gordon's time in China is largely a mystery. Family records note his injury in the Boxer riots but no reason for his visit there has been found. The beheadings of his cousin Christina, her husband William and their son Alexander in 1900 are a matter of public record.

Gordon worked in the foreign concession in Yokohama. His name appears on the passenger lists of ships arriving and leaving from Japanese ports and he is known to have been employed by Abenheim Brothers. Rick Taniguchi and Katsuyoshi, Midori and Yukie Yokoyama have kindly helped to build a picture of Gordon's stay in Japan which would have been impossible for me to do given the language difficulties in researching documents there.

Mary McElhone nursed Gordon in Petrograd. He had fallen ill with double pneumonia on the train and died several days later. In a touching letter sent from the British Nursing Home to Gordon's mother in November 1917, she writes,

> *The Russian sister who was with him was fearfully upset by his death and says she feels quite certain he went straight to Heaven, he had a smile and a cheery word up to the very last.*

Meeting Leslie Chandler's son, Errol, was an unexpected boost to my lines of enquiry. He generously shared information about his father, freely acknowledging that much about him remains unknown even to his closest family. Leslie's involvement with the funeral arrangements in Petrograd, and his visit to Dr John Dickson in Huddersfield soon after Gordon died, are the marks of a caring person.

David Verguson kindly sent me a photograph of Gordon's name inscribed on the war memorial at Oakes Baptist Church, Lindley.

My brother Michael and cousins William Gee, Andrew Lloyd-Williams and Sue Woodd made helpful suggestions for correcting and improving a draft manuscript. Sara Donaldson was a formidable copyeditor. I am grateful to them all. I would also like to record my thanks to Axel Ienna for encouraging me to write this story and to Rowan Somerville for his guidance.

The story I have written is a mixture of fact and fiction. I offer an unreserved apology to the relatives of any individual I may have portrayed inaccurately, such was not my intention. Many characters, including Ling, Vladimir and James, are products of my imagination, as are most of the events.

I take responsibility for factual errors.

Finally, I must thank Gordon himself for taking me on this journey.

Printed in Great Britain
by Amazon